# Friends and Lovers

# Friends and Lovers

Joan Smith

ROBERT HALE · LONDON

ISBN 978-0-7090-7927-9

Robert Hale Limited
Clerkenwell House
Clerkenwell Green
London EC1R 0HT

www.halebooks.com

2 4 6 8 10 9 7 5 3 1

Typeset in 11/15pt Souvenir
by Derek Doyle & Associates, Shaw Heath
Printed in Great Britain by the MPG Books Group, Bodmin and King's Lynn

# Chapter One

We made our big mistake in letting Mr Everett look at our box stairs. He fancies himself something of a gentleman cum architect, you see. He is neither one nor the other, I promise you. He is a retired merchant, who had a garish mansion built to his own design just outside of Reading, when he gave up his building-supply company in London two years ago. Mr Everett has masses of money, which he wishes to share, along with his name, with some undemanding gentlewoman. He is a lively soul, as common as dirt, whom I would be happy to have for a friend, if only he would not insist on being more than a friend.. Lately, he has begun assuming some of the privileges of a lover. He drops in on us with regularity three times a week, though Oakdene, his home, is some six miles away. On his last visit, Mama made the dreadful error of saying she disliked our box stairs. We always discuss some aspect of building with Mr Everett. He hasn't an idea of conversation beyond lumber and hardware.

'They are so dark, you know,' she mentioned, 'and the ceiling too low for safety. *I* do not bump my head to be sure [Mama is barely five feet high], and Gwendolyn has trained herself to duck, but any chance visitor is sure to give himself a knock. Quite dangerous, really.'

'My stairhead at Oakdene gives a tall man a clearance of six feet,' he answered. 'I raised the ceiling beams two feet higher than Skanner had them in our design. It cost me something in the neighborhood of a thousand pounds to do it throughout the house, but I did not want anything meager about Oakdene.' He usually gives a more precise price, in pounds and pence, for his undertakings and possessions.

'Ours gives a short woman a clearance of an inch,' I replied. You can only match Everett by claiming an underabundance. There is no point vying in square acres of floor space, miles of garden, quality of materials, or anything else.

'May I have a look at it for you, Mrs Harris?' he asked, already on his feet and strutting toward the staircase. He is tall, rather awkward in motion. It sounds absurd, but I don't believe his knees work. At least they do not bend when he walks. He struts about with his legs perfectly stiff. Outside of this awkward gait, he is not unhandsome in appearance for a man in his forties. He has dark hair, just silvering at the temples, jolly brown eyes, an unexceptionable nose, and large teeth. His wardrobe follows the extravagant taste of his mansion – high shirt points, wide shoulders, nipped waist, bright waistcoats, everything brand new and in the highest kick of fashion.

Mama tossed me a helpless, defeated look behind his retreating back, then arose to follow him into the hall, while I taggled behind. He stood on the bottom stair, craning his neck up, then down and all around. He could not resist tapping the paneling of the outer wall and saying, 'Spruce,' in a derogatory way. 'Stained to resemble dark oak, but these walls are spruce.'

We accepted this chastisement mutely. We knew from past conversations his love of oak. 'May I?' he asked next as he ran up the stairs and back down again, carefully laying his shoulders and head back to avoid banging his forehead on the oak, or possibly stained spruce, beam, that has been banging tall gentlemen's heads for over two hundred years.

'It is your first-story floor that is too low,' he told us after he had descended. 'That is to say, your ground-story ceiling is too low. What you want is another foot or two of elevation.'

'Short of tearing the house apart, we are not likely to get it,' I pointed out, taking a step back to the sitting room. No steps followed me. He remained in place, staring up at the mischievous beam, approximately fifteen inches in diameter, that acts as a lintel across the ceiling of the stairhead.

'I don't see why that beam could not be cut away six inches,' Mama said hopefully. 'Surely such a huge thing is not necessary, only to hold the walls apart.'

He smiled on her kindly but could not suppress a chuckle at her naiveté. Our innocence in architectural matters was a source of continuing amusement to him. We were treated to a lengthy and very obscure treatise on building, in which weight-bearing members, pounds per square inch of weight carried, the inefficiency of lintels versus Roman arches, and the general decrepitude of our lumber each made up a part.

'So you see there is no way you could cut your beam in half,' he terminated, giving it a tap with his knuckles.

'It does not *sound* hollow, does it?' Mama asked.

'Not hollow. I did not say hollow, ma'am, but riddled with dry rot,' he corrected. '*Practically* hollow, where the termites have feasted on it any time these last centuries. You would have the ceiling tumbling down on your head, unless you reinforced the supporting walls with a pair of columns, with perhaps a hammer beam atop . . . You really haven't room for a set of columns,' he added sadly. 'I have all sorts of columns and pilasters at Oakdene.'

Mama accepted his dictum. 'I daresay nothing can be done about the box around the stairs either,' she said.

It was really the box panels that annoyed her most. A box stairs is a dark thing, its side wall cutting off all light from below.

There is a portion just past the turn in the stairs where the beam occurs that is pitch black, even at high noon. Mama and I have often discussed the desirability of removing the panel and putting in a pretty railing and spindles to replace it. I cannot think it would be a huge job either, but it was never done. We are only tenants at the cottage. The owner is a fiend for leaving it exactly as it is. 'A gem of Elizabethan architecture' is his manner of describing it in the guide books to famous estates.

'Now, that is a different matter entirely,' he assured us. 'These spruce veneers could be ripped out in the twinkling of a bedpost. Not more than half an inch thick,' he added, tapping them. 'You would want to finish off the end of the steps that would be exposed, slip in a few rods, hammer a railing on top, and there you are. Nothing to it.'

'I am happy to hear it,' Mama said, nodding her satisfaction.

'Now may we return to the sitting room and our tea?' I asked impatiently. The improvement of the stairs is only a topic for conversation with us. We knew perfectly well nothing would ever be done.

Everett strutted forward to accompany me, leaving Mama behind to stare in a bemused way at the spruce veneers.

'So, when do you want me to do it?' was his next speech. Mama entered as he made it. He turned his question to her. 'I was just asking your daughter when it would be convenient for me to come and fix up that dark stair-corner for you.'

'Oh, we have not decided for sure!' she exclaimed, aghast at this decisive way of going on.

'What is to decide? You said it has annoyed you forever. I could have my men do it in a day. Skanner still comes out from town once a week, and I have three carpenters finishing up my attics. A very pretty carved cherry trim is going around the wainscotting. I do not think the *attics* merit oak.'

Even a carved cherry trim in an attic may strike you as

unnecessary. It will not be out of place at Oakdene. Every inch of wood in the house is carved, most of it painted and gilded on top of that. The elaborate parquet floors did escape carving. They were designed by an Italian artist, not in plain triangles or rectangles, but to form peacocks, unicorns, and other handsome animals, much larger than life, one to a room. They caused considerable excitement in the neighborhood before he succumbed to the lure of Persian carpets to cover them.

'You forget the cottage does not belong to us, Mr Everett,' I said. 'We only have it on lease from Lord Menrod.'

'Why, he is your brother-in-law, is he not? What objection could he have, so long as he is not asked to bear the expense?' He held up his callused hand, palm toward us, to signal we were not to object to his next speech, nor to interrupt him. 'I mean to do it as a present, pay for the whole. I can get lumber at wholesale prices, and have three carpenters sitting on their thumbs half the day. They might as well be working. They cost me enough. Three pounds a week. No, I tell a lie. One of them is learning the trade. I get him for less.'

'We could not consider it,' I said at once.

'Menrod is not our brother-in-law, either,' Mama added. 'He is only a connection. My elder daughter married his younger brother, but there was never any closeness between our families. Lord Peter and Hettie went out to India right after they were married, you see, which is why we never had anything to do with Menrod. Well, he is not often in residence in any case. He was traveling for two years, all over the continent. He has another estate he goes to in winter, and is in London for the Season. We are not close enough that we like to ask him about it.'

'*I'll* ask him,' Everett said, pushing on to overcome every obstacle. 'I don't suppose the fellow is a fool. He will be happy enough to have his house fixed up at no expense to himself.'

'We cannot accept your offer. Thank you very much, Mr Everett,' I said firmly. 'Menrod is very fussy about the cottage, because of its being an authentic Elizabethan home.'

'Very kind of you,' Mama added, 'but impossible.'

There was no trusting the face he wore. I feared he would land a load of lumber at our door the next morning, so warned him against it before he left.

'I would not do it without Menrod's permission,' he agreed. Knowing Menrod was not home, I felt easier.

The lumber did not arrive for four days. On a Saturday in March it came, accompanied by Mr Everett, to oversee its placement. Skanner came in with him, to test the inadequacy of our beam first, then to look at the box stairs. 'Tamarack,' Skanner said, squeezing the huge and offensive beam. Bits fell off in his hands. 'It is here to stay.'

'Even with all the dry rot?' Mama asked hopefully.

'Tamarack is as strong as steel,' he informed us. 'You would think to look at it you could pull it apart with your bare hands. You would wear out your chisel before you made any headway with it. Screwdriver,' He said to a boy who had come with them to carry Mr Skanner's tools.

He stuck it under the quarter-round molding of the box panel and pried hard. The molding came off, scattering a few bits of splinters on the floor. Next he applied the screwdriver to the panel itself. It too was very obliging in the matter of leaving its ancient home. They encountered all manner of obstacle after the first simple steps.

'They knew how to build in the old days,' Skanner said, pointing the screwdriver at an ugly mess of raw lumber ends, rough hewn, that formed the edge of the steps. They were supported by whole tree trunks underneath. Elephants could have used those steps without breaking them.

'What we'll do is just put a half panel up to the tops of the steps, with a facing to hold the spindles, and the bannister on top.'

'Mr Everett, we cannot do this without Menrod's permission,' I said. 'Please, hammer back on the panel.'

The callused hand came up to silence me. 'I have been in touch with Lord Menrod. Wrote to him in London,' he assured me.

'He approved?'

'He had no objection. Why should he?'

'He objected very strenuously to our changing the thatched roof.'

'That is on the outside, where everyone sees it. He does not care about the inside, but only wants you to be comfortable,' Mr Everett explained.

This did not sound like Menrod. 'It would be nice, dear,' Mama said.

There was a whispered colloquy behind the men's backs, as we quickly agreed we could spare a few pounds of our allowance to pay for the expense of it. When they had finished deciding the manner of.doing the job, I told Mr Everett we would insist on paying for it.

He smiled, revealing his big square teeth. 'Of course, Miss Harris, if you insist,' he said, so docilely that I knew he had no intention of taking the money when the time came.

'How much will it cost?' I asked.

'For you, two pennies,' he said, laughing.

'Mr Skanner – how much will this job cost?' I asked.

'Ten guineas should cover it,' he replied.

It does not sound an overwhelming sum, but to two ladies living on the interest of a rector's capital, it was considerable. Of course we got our house for an old song, because of our connection with Menrod. My late father had been in charge of three of his lordship's livings, with curates under him in two of them. It is a practice much disparaged nowadays, but *every* career has its upward route, and if a clergyman has not the ability or desire to rise up through the echelon of Dean to Bishop, and so on, then he will usually widen his activities and increase his income by swallowing up a few livings in the near neighborhood. We had some small capital, whose interest allowed us to maintain the dignity of our own carriage and a few servants. With the house thrown in so cheaply, we hobbled along pretty well, and would even manage to pay the ten guineas for the improved staircase ourselves. Everett must not be allowed to do it; he would think he had got a lien on my body if he paid.

'To whom do I make the payment, to Mr Everett or yourself?' I asked Skanner.

'I work for Mr Everett,' he answered. 'It has nothing to do with me. Work it out between you.'

Everett was smiling on me in such a disgustingly doting way I wanted to hit him with the screwdriver.

'We'll just draw up a design for the new spindles and railing, then, and present it tomorrow for your approval,' Everett told me.

The 'tomorrow' he had slipped in slyly; we more usually had a day off between his visits. I realized at once he meant to make it an excuse to take over our house entirely, to be running tame, like the beau he fancied himself.

'Take your time, sir,' I said coolly. 'Do not feel it necessary to come to us every day, to oversee the job.'

The doting smile widened till I had to search for a word to describe it. 'Fond' did not begin to do it justice. It was closer to possessive, and pleased with its possession.

He did not heed my hint, but returned the next day with a design I disliked intensely. I knew those dragon heads and claws would cost a fortune to have carved, to say nothing of looking very ugly and anachronistic in an Elizabethan house.

'They are much too fancy,' I told him, not wishing to say in so many words he was a fool with extremely poor taste. 'Just a plain round spindle, with perhaps a few rings cut into the shaft of it, as most spindles you see in other homes have. I doubt it is Elizabethan, but it will not stand out like a sore thumb.'

He was back the next day with more sketches, each done by his own hand, colored in water color, signed in black ink, like Skanner's sketches for Oakdene. A mansion rated such lavish treatment; surely a staircase did not, but it was intended as a compliment to me. The smile left no doubt on that score. The dragons and lotus blossoms had dwindled to snakes and apples, but still they were not rings cut into a plain spindle. 'Like this,' I said impatiently, roughly sketching down my meaning.

'Happen you're right,' he said, nodding his acquiescence. 'There is no point trying to make anything of this little place, when all is said and done. And why should we, eh?'

'Why indeed? Let Menrod do it, if he wants something fancier. The spindles will do excellently for Mama and me.'

'That was not my meaning, Miss Harris,' he ventured boldly.

Three visits, three days hard running, had done something awful to his encroaching manners. 'I think you know where there is a more gracious home waiting to receive you and your mother, whenever you feel so inclined.'

That was his proposal. I looked out the window and pretended not to understand his meaning. 'The chiffchaffs are back early this year,' I said. I arose and walked to the window to admire these dainty warblers. He was not two steps behind me, hardly one. He put a hand on my shoulder, causing me to flinch.

Before he could expand on his invitation to remove to Oakdene, our attention was diverted to the garden beneath the tree where rested the chiff-chaffs. There was a black cat slinking behind the bushes, and not far behind the cat was our female factotum, Mrs Pudge, flapping a tea towel at the cat's tail, and ordering him away from her birds. Her angry speech was inaudible through the closed window, but her appearance was comical enough to arrest Everett's proposal in mid-flight.

Mrs Pudge is a short woman, about the same height as my mother. She is very stout, with a fantastic top-knot of sandish-gray hair. She wears voluminous aprons to protect her gown from the cooking jobs. She has bright blue eyes, an infant's little button of a nose, and a chin about five inches long, which she now wagged at the old tomcat who comes on marauding missions from Menrod Manor, its home, a few miles north of us. I don't know whether the cat has a name; to Mrs Pudge it is known as 'that devil cat.' Mrs Pudge has a genteel white female kitten, rapidly becoming mature, which is a stronger inducement to the tomcat than the birds ever were. This pet is called Lady, and is the only member of the household, including her spouse, on whom our housekeeper bestows the least affection. I believe it is her fear that the devil cat will molest Lady that causes her special rancor toward this animal, for really she is not all that fond of birds, though she calls them 'her' birds, in a proprietary way, and tosses a handful of crumbs to them when she is in the mood, or when her pile of dried bread overflows its container.

'Foolish old malkin,' Mr Everett said, unhappy at being interrupted in his mission.

I squirmed out past him to the safety of the chair closest the door, where I called to Mr Pudge to send Mama in for approval of the stairway design. I was safe from Mr Everett's ardor till his next visit. After Mama approved the design, it was arranged that the three carpenters would come the next morning at nine to begin their job. Everett did not say he would accompany them, neither did I wish to show any interest in whether he came or not, so did not ask, but I had the most sinking apprehension that he would.

# Chapter Two

𝓜y mother and I have only been living in our present home for three years. It is a charming place, as seen from outside. It bears a strong resemblance to Anne Hathaway's cottage, complete with timber and plaster facade, some ornamental brickwork on the sides, a thatched roof, and leaded windows. All this charm is much prettier to look at than to live in. Rodents are much attracted to the thatched roof. Rain does not evaporate so quickly from thatch as from slate, either. It is damp, and the damp invades the upper story of the house, bringing with it a certain musty odor that is pervasive. The leaded windows, though they sparkle like diamonds, are not so large as windows ought to be. Insufficient light enters at every room. In winter, our rooms look strangely circular, the corners lost in shadows.

We have tried a dozen stunts to overcome the gloom of the interior. Our most effective remedy to date is to paint any nonvaluable piece of furniture light and bright. A pale lemon yellow was our choice. Many cabinets, tables, and the dining room chairs now stand out starkly against the age-dimmed paneling of the rooms, more starkly than I had hoped.

When my father died, three years ago, it was necessary for us to vacate the rectory to make way for the new incumbent. As Hettie had married Lord Peter some years before, Menrod took into his head to do something for us, and gave us the cottage at a nominal cost. The place is called Lady Anne's cottage, and sits on one corner of his vast estate. I was disappointed he had not let us have one of his other homes instead. There is a fine Dower House, but he has his dowager step-mother living there; there is also a very nice gate-house, but the gatekeeper lives there. There are any number of tenant farms, all inhabited by tenant farmers. The only other one we might have come into was a gracious, modern red brick home just at the south edge of his estate, facing the Kennet River. He moved his summer mistress into it at the same time he gave us Lady Anne's cottage.

I let on to Mama I am as happy as may be here, but in fact, I have had a plan of escape brewing for a year now, ever since we heard word from India of Lord Peter's and Hettie's death in a boating accident. That was a great tragedy for us. Hettie was my only sister, and my dearest friend. Though she had been in India already for seven years, I felt as close to her as ever. She was a marvelous correspondent. I can close my eyes and see her home there, know all the bizarre entertainments she enjoyed, her new friends, the Indian customs. When she had her first child, she called her Gwendolyn, after me. Two years later, she had a son, named Ralph, after Peter's father. It had been agreed between us sisters, though never revealed to Mama, that I would go to India to be with her for her next lying-in. She hinted at a surfeit of gentlemen looking for an English wife. I don't know that I would have been happy *living* in India, but I would dearly have loved to see it. I have never been farther east than to London, forty miles away. Living on this small island, surrounded by water, I have never seen the sea. I had a holiday sixty miles west of here, at Bath, one summer when my mother was feeling poorly. An invalid mother is not the jolliest travelling companion.

My plan for escaping Lady Anne's cottage centers around Hettie's children. They are to be shipped home to England. I thought we would have seen them before now, but it was necessary to wait till some suitable person could be found to accompany them home, then to arrange passage, and so on. If I were Menrod, I think I would have bestirred myself to go after them, as he enjoys trotting all around the globe, but his lordship did not see fit to do so. He was busy restocking his coverts at the time. When they do eventually return, it is my plan and ardent hope they might be placed with Mama and me. Lord Peter had some money, so a house will be adequately provided. I will be aunt, friend, companion, governess, nanny – whatever they require. It strikes me as a marvelous plan.

Mrs Pudge once told me, in a fit of poetry induced by my having lost a beau, that God forgets to be gracious to some of his flock. I feel I am one of His forgotten ones. He showered the daughters' share of beauty mostly on Hettie, forgetting to give me my dimples and curly hair. He had forgotten to give me either a fortune or a husband with one. What He gave me instead was a fairly short temper, and a reason to wonder why He had bothered to create me at all. Now the wisdom of His plan was revealed. This was why I had been born, to be here when the children needed me. I had a purpose, a need to fill at last.

The only remaining item to be settled is to discuss it with Menrod, who will be in charge of managing their monies. No doubt he will be greatly relieved we are willing to tend the children. As he likes to be free to dart to Scotland for the trout fishing, Brighton for the water, the Cotswold Hills for hunting, London for the Season, and the continent for chasing women, he will be happy to know the children have a good home.

The long-awaited letter telling of their arrival came the second day Everett and the carpenters were at the cottage working on the box stairs. To that time, they had made a colossal racket and mess, disassembling the wall panels. Everett has some pieces of wood he is drawing a design on for the bottom panel, to hide the rough step-ends. This occupies most of his time, and all of our dining room table, which is where he has elected to do his calculations and design. Mama and I now take all our meals in the breakfast parlor, which is no more than a corner nook by the window, overlooking the rose garden.

The letter was written by a Mr Enberg, a friend of Peter's, telling us he was leaving India with the children the next week, to return to England on the East India Company ship. The letter was three months old, which made it probable they would be arriving within the next week or so. It had taken Hettie eighty-five days to get there. He would take the children to London. He had also written to Menrod, who would presumably meet them there, as he had not asked us to.

After we had done rejoicing, our next business was to discover whether Menrod had received his letter and would be in London to meet the children. I had no idea where he might be in March. Late April would certainly see him in London for the Season, with darts to Newmarket and Epsom for the races. I had some inkling he might be at one of the smaller race meets, the hurdles at Dover or Warwick, perhaps, for he was a keen horseman.

'Let us go up to Dower House and speak to Lady Menrod,' I suggested. 'She will know where he is.'

'Mr Everett knows – he wrote him in London, did he not?'

'Indeed he did, but that was a whole week ago. I'll speak to him, see if Menrod mentioned his plans. If he is not in London, we will have to go and meet the children, Mama.'

'Oh, dear!' she exclaimed, aghast at the idea. We live less than fifty miles from the city, but do not make the trip oftener than once every two or three years. We have not been there since my father's death.

I went on the fly into the hallway to put the question to Mr Everett. 'I have no notion where he might be,' he answered.

'He did not mention how long he would be staying in London?'

'Why would he tell *me*? I have never met the man.'

'You wrote to him. In his reply, I thought he might have said something.'

'I had no reply to my letter. That looks as though he was not in the city at all, does it not?'

'Had no reply?' I asked, staring. 'You said he approved of the alterations! You don't mean you have gone tearing the house apart without his consent? He is as fussy as may be about the cottage, because of its age and authenticity. He wants it kept as a gem of Elizabethan architecture. He would not hear of having the thatch removed and shingles put on last year, when the mice were driving us to distraction.'

'I told him I was doing it. If he disliked it, he would have written.'

'How could he write, if he didn't have your letter? Oh, Mr Everett, you had better hammer those panels back on immediately.'

'I had them carted away to my place and burned, out back where the lads are clearing away all the bits and pieces from my own construction. I did not want to leave you with the mess.'

'You have saddled me with a greater mess than a few pieces of wood. I dread to think what Menrod will have to say about this.'

'Now, Miss Harris, don't fret your pretty head. I will handle Lord Menrod if he cuts up stiff over getting a dandy new set of stairs at no cost.'

'I most particularly wanted to have him in a good mood, too,' I said.

This had to be explained to the inquisitive architect. He was displeased at the intelligence. 'You mean to *live* with the young-sters, you say?' he asked, frowning.

'My own sister's children – what could be more natural?'

'Did she leave them in your custody?'

'I am not at all sure those legal arrangements had been made. Both Peter and Hettie were so young, they were not thinking of their death yet, or planning for it. But there is no one else except Menrod and us. He will not want them.'

'I'd make him take them if I were you, Miss Harris.'

'One does not *make* Lord Menrod do anything he dislikes. He will dislike very much to have the care of two small children. Of course we shall take them.'

'I don't know that I fancy . . . though Oakdene is a great, rambling place. Eighty rooms in all. No, I tell a lie. There are seventy-eight. Still, they would not be underfoot. . . .' he said, in a musing way that showed clearly he had not given up his pursuit of me.

'I do not plan to billet them on *you*, Mr Everett. They will stay with my mother and myself,' I answered sharply, and whirled away. Then I suddenly whirled back. 'Please restore that staircase to as close a likeness of its former condition as possible, as soon as possible.'

'I'll do better than that. You'll be proud of the job, Miss Harris,' he answered with a low bow.

I was too distraught to read the ominous overtones in his speech. To a man who considered Oakdene beautiful, what grotesquerie would constitute a job to be proud of?

I donned my pelisse and bonnet and went straight up to the Dower House to converse with Lady Menrod, in an effort to discover Menrod's whereabouts. Old Lord Menrod had married a youngish widow in his dotage, and died within a few years. The heir never liked his stepmother. He had her shipped into the Dower House within six months of his father's death, where she had remained ever since. The rest of the parish took no exception to the lady. She was now in her fifties, an elegant and rather shy dame, who made no demands whatsoever on her stepson.

She was entertaining a guest when I arrived in her saloon. Lady Althea Costigan is some kin to the dowager countess, though not a close relative. She lives in London but spends enough time in our neighborhood that she is considered half an inhabitant. She is a little older than myself – thirtyish, to judge by the fine lines etching their way in at the corners of her eyes. She has pretty auburn hair and striking green eyes. It is mainly her figure for which she is remembered. It is of that fullness just a shade short of stout, most often described as voluptuous.

I explained my business to them and waited eagerly to hear what they could tell me. 'I have no idea where he may be,' the Dowager said, with a noticeable lack of enthusiasm.

'When I spoke to him last week in London, he said he was off to the selling races at Brighton, to look out for a filly,' Lady Althea told me.

'Had he heard from Mr Enberg yet?' I asked, for if he had, he would of course return to London to meet the ship.

'He did not mention it if he had,' she answered.

'Then he had not heard. He would have mentioned such an important matter,' I thought aloud.

Lady Althea and her hostess looked unconvinced. 'He might,' the former agreed, 'but if I were you, Miss Harris, I would just run along to London to be sure someone is there to receive the children.'

It sounded so miraculously simple – 'just run along to London.' Running off to London I could not do alone, and to move Mama in that direction would take one of Mr Congreve's rockets at least. Then too, there was Mr Everett, ripping the house apart during our absence. I had no accurate idea of when the ship was to arrive. Suppose I got there a week early, and had to put up at an expensive hotel during the interim. The alternative was to send Mr Pudge. I could think of no other. It was not the problem of my hostess, however, so I accepted a cup of tea and made a brief social visit of it.

'Don't vex yourself, Miss Harris,' Lady Menrod advised. 'My stepson will handle it. If he did not receive the letter himself, his man of business will have done so, and made all the arrangements. Menrod does not leave anything to chance. He is quite a perfectionist.'

'He will be at the Manor for the children's arrival, to see them,' Lady Althea added, while a calculating light shone in her eyes.

'You may depend upon it. Menrod always does the right thing. Maybe that will convince you to prolong your visit, Althea,' Lady Menrod suggested, with a twinkle in her dark eyes.

I had not realized before that moment that Lady Althea came to visit her relative with any other end than friendship in view. The last speech awakened me to the realization she was throwing her cap at Menrod. A perfectly suitable match it would be, too. I wondered she had not pulled it off long ago. She must have timed her visits poorly, to have failed in her goal.

I was so preoccupied with worrying about meeting the children, that my attention wandered from their conversation. As soon as politely possible, I took my leave, to return home and discuss with Mama what ought to be done. She was all for letting Menrod handle it, but the awful suspicion would intrude that Menrod was not infallible. Suppose he did *not* handle it, then what? Were we to leave two children stranded on the docks of London?

Mr Everett, running back and forth from stairs to dining

room table, caught the gist of our conversation. Being as encroaching as a mushroom, he did not hesitate a moment to offer his services.

'I'll just nip down to London and deliver the youngsters for you,' he told us.

'That would give us time to prepare the nursery rooms for them, to air the beds, and make sure everything is ready,' Mama said at once.

'I would not like to have them met by a stranger,' I objected.

'No, really! Stranger indeed! You are too hard on me,' Everett declared.

'You are a stranger to them yourself, Gwendolyn. We all are,' Mama pointed out, quite correctly.

Mr Everett was hardly of a nature to frighten them out of their wits. He was friendly, fatherly, in a way. The trip represented such a high hurdle to me that in the end I allowed myself to be talked into accepting yet another favor from Mr Everett.

'Very likely Menrod will take care of them,' I reminded him, for to have him fighting with his lordship or his emissary in front of the children was a fearful conjecture. 'If he is there, or if he has sent his man, you need do no more than say good day to them. It is a hard trip to take, with a possibility of its being entirely unnecessary.'

'It happens I had to go anyway. It is nothing but a pleasure to me, to be able to serve you.'

I feared he was telling another lie, but he did not correct himself on this occasion. Later I went to check out his progress on the box stairs. Nothing had been done, though a large sheet of wood lay on the dining table, the outline of the steps drawn on it with a black grease pencil, ready for sawing.

'Remember, the panel is not to be cut, Mr Everett. We want it right back up to the ceiling,' I reminded him. 'Can the carpenters go ahead with it during your absence?'

'Certainly they can, and will. It will be done before you can say one, two, three.'

All his help earned him an invitation to take potluck that evening for dinner. It was the first time he had sat down to a formal meal with us. Mrs Pudge was in the boughs with us for asking him. Ever since Hettie married Lord Peter, she has had ideas above our station. She thinks we are royalty, or nobility, at least.

'What will his lordship think of you entertaining commoners?' she asked, a fire burning in her blue eyes, her chin wagging.

About twenty years ago, my father gave her a Psalter for Christmas. It, her Bible, and the Pilgrim's Progress are her library, sitting in state on her bed table, when they are not in her hands. She has them nearly by heart, and is liberal with her condemnations against the ungodly, and the unnoble.

'How should he know, Mrs Pudge?' I asked.

'The scandal mongers won't be slow to trot to him with the news. Bad enough the heathen sits down for tea three times a week, without having a place at our table.'

She does not have that degree of respect for Lord Menrod that the above would indicate. He too is frequently amongst the godless, but she has learned the trick of dividing her enemies against each other, in an effort to bring us all to justice.

'They will have a long trot, for no one knows where he is.'

'Aye, a long trek, whetting their tongues like a sword all the way. Will he be carving the roast, your Mr Everett, or will I have Pudge to do it for you, as usual?'

'Let Pudge do it. It might put ideas in Mr Everett's head, to sit carving the roast at the head of the table.'

'You'll never let him sit in the master's place!' she gasped.

'No, no – it was only a manner of speaking. Put him at Mama's right.'

'It's a sad and sorrowful day,' she grieved. 'You'll be a proverb in the countryside, taking your mutton with the creature. As to them steps he is destroying in the front hallway, I hope you can keep the sight from Lord Menrod, or he'll cast you into the desert, without a bone to gnaw on.'

'Have you anymore abominations to threaten us with, or will you go now and get the dining table cleared away, Mrs Pudge?'

She glared once, then strode off, her chin waggling about heathens coming into their inheritance.

# Chapter Three

$\mathcal{M}$r Everett left the next morning for London. My mother and myself spent the day on thorns, running to the front window every half hour to see if they were coming up the road yet. We began our intermittent vigil about noon, not many minutes after Mr Everett would have reached the city. We knew it was impossible they could be back home yet, but our eagerness would not be satisfied till we had looked out the window just once more. We were still looking long after the sun had set, in hopes of spotting carriage lights. Had it not been for the extra work around the house preparing rooms for the children, we would have been totally distracted. We roasted up a joint in their honor, then returned nine-tenths of it to the kitchen after we finished our evening meal.

Next day, the procedure was repeated, the running to the door or window every half hour. When the postman arrived, I realized what a monster of inconsideration I was. There was a dutiful letter from Mr Everett explaining there was no Indiaman in the harbor. He would remain in London till the end of the week, awaiting the children's arrival. A long and expensive stay in London on the *possibility* that he might be required to meet the relatives of a woman who half despised him, if the whole truth were stated.

I answered by return post that he must under no circumstance put himself to so much inconvenience. He was to deliver a note in person to Menrod's London residence, and be assured it was read, understood, and that some of Menrod's household would meet the children. His letter posted the day before did not preclude the possibility of his arriving in person later that day. The vigil was maintained till nearly midnight. Early the next morning, it was resumed. *Surely* they would come today!

By noon, I never wanted to see the front window, the mulberry tree in the front yard, or the stone road down to the main road again. I took my watering can to the little conservatory that is attached to the west wing of the cottage, to tend my plants. They had been miserably neglected. Even in the moist atmosphere of the conservatory, the earth around many of them had turned crumbly from thirst. My philodendron had brown tips on its leaves, and my favorite dracaena wilted with fatigue. I put on my smock and busied myself tending my friends, filling the water racks over the fire boxes, whose function was to lend moisture to the air. I pruned and pinched and watered, losing myself to worldly cares for an hour.

There is some magical enchantment in gardening. Had Lady Anne's cottage not had this little conservatory attached, I would never have discovered it, for I never took any interest in plants before moving here. While I worked over my pots and boxes, a feeling of deep peace descended upon me. Daydreams unfolded in my head, of a halcyon future in which I played mother to my niece and nephew. I had an idea how the children looked, from pencil sketches Hettie had sent home shortly before her death. I knew Gwen would be six now, Ralph four. Gwen favored the Harris family in her physical makeup. She had Hettie's and my own fair skin and gray eyes. Like us, her hair was an indeterminate shade of light brown that came close to blond in summer, darkening to a less attractive shade in winter. God's graciousness had been passed along from mother to daughter, endowing the latter with the dimples and curls that avoided me. Ralph more closely resembled his father, having darker-brown hair and brown eyes. His waywardness was occasionally mentioned, and blamed on his being of the male sex, but between friends and family, we admitted he might have inherited a little something of unstable temperament from his father as well. No matter, he was young, and I would train him up to be a proper gentleman.

I arranged a fairly idyllic life for us all. Menrod would give Ralph a pony on his sixth birthday. He would also want to send him away to a public school later on, but my idyll did not extend so far into the future. I thought of the nearer term, when we would be into a more comfortable house than the dilapidated cottage. Gwen would come to view me as very much of a substitute mother. When you reach twenty-five and have no family of your own, it is a rare gift indeed to be given a child who bears not only your family's blood, but even your own name. I knew as surely as my dracaena was wilting to death that I would love the children, and formed the firm resolution they would be made to love me in return. I would have children, even if a husband was denied me.

'He's here,' Mrs Pudge hollered from the conservatory door. She held her cooking apron in her hands, indicating she had ripped it off and run up from the kitchen to get the door, which told me Pudge was busy in the yard, fighting with the roses. They share the duties of butler in this fashion.

'Are the children with Mr Everett?' I asked, removing my gloves and struggling out of my smock.

'It's not Everett. It's *him*. Lord Menrod.'

'Menrod? What is he doing here? Has he brought the children?'

'No, he's alone, and he says he's in a hurry, so you had better come as you are.'

I brushed my hair back, tucking in a loose strand, and wishing I might take time to nip upstairs to tidy myself before greeting him. We do not often have the honor of greeting a lord at our cottage door. I also wished I had thought to put a chair or table before the destroyed staircase. The carpenters had left, awaiting Everett's return from London. I begged them to finish up the job in *some* manner, but they were worriesomely coy, which inclined me to fear Everett was buying some hideous materials or ornament for the job.

I hastened to the sitting room, to find Menrod standing in the middle of the floor, with his quizzing glass raised to examine the fireplace. He turned his austere, gaunt face toward me. Menrod is tall and thin. He dresses with no frills, but all his materials and tailoring are of the finest. He is dark-complexioned, like all his family. 'You have changed the fire irons here,' he said in an accusing tone. His manners are not so fine as his tailoring. 'The tongs, the poker, the shovel – where are they?'

'They fell apart from age. Their handles were made of wood, you know. It is not easy to tend a fire with handleless tools. Have you seen the children?'

'Where did you put the pieces? I know a blacksmith who repairs valuable old artifacts. Those brass-handled things clash with the rest of the house. I'll have the wooden handles replaced.'

'I don't know where the bits and pieces are. Have you seen the children?' I repeated, becoming exasperated at his nit-picking.

'I hope your mother has them put away safely. I told her when I let her use this house, I wanted nothing changed. Those items are antiques.'

My mind flew to the antique stairs, fast on their way to join-
ing us in the nineteenth century, but it was only a fleeting
thought, a rush of relief that he had not noticed them. 'Will you
answer me?' I asked, my voice rising with vexation. 'Have you
seen the children?'

He gave one last frown at the new fire irons before honoring
me with a direct look: I was struck, as I always was upon a close
view of him, at how cold his eyes were. Brown eyes are usually
friendly – not Menrod's. The thinly arched brows had something to do with it; they gave him a disdainful expression, which
his thin lips did not lessen. He brought the frost into the room
with him. He lifted an elegant hand to indicate I was to be
seated, before more discussion. I flounced to the closest chair
and plumped down, undaintily. He strolled to the sofa and
lowered himself as carefully and gracefully as any lady. Then he
threw one leg over the other, admired his fawn trousers a
moment, and finally answered.

'Of course I have seen them. That is why I am here – to tell
you I have brought them home to Menrod Manor. I thought you
would like to know they are safely home. You are welcome to
come up and see them sometime, if you like. Or I will be happy
to bring them to you for a visit, if you prefer. I will be home for
a few days.'

My excitement to learn they had arrived safely all the way
from India robbed me of the greater part of my perceptive
faculties. I read nothing forbidding in the latter part of his
speech. 'Oh, I am so glad, so relieved. Did you meet their boat
at London?'

'Certainly not. I am much too busy. I left word at the ship-
ping office to be notified as soon as the ship was sighted. My
man went to the dock to bring them to my London residence.
They are both in good health, have withstood the journey well,

and appear to be recovering from the loss of their parents. I thought you would be happy to hear it.'

'I am delighted. I wish you had brought them down with you. You cannot imagine how anxious I am to meet them.'

'Are you indeed?' he asked, a mobile brow rising. 'I imagined that, like myself, you would view their arrival as more of a nuisance than anything else. I would have brought them down yesterday, had I realized your eagerness to see them.'

'Yesterday? You mean they have been at the Manor for a whole day, and you are only *now* letting us know?'

'Yes, we would have been here sooner, but I took a few days off to show them the sights of London before bringing them home.'

'Well, upon my word! You might have let us know what was going on. Here I have sent poor Mr Everett all the way to London on a fool's errand, to meet them in case you were not aware of their coming.'

'How should I not be aware? I have known for six months of their coming. It was arranged through a friend of mine who went out to India to work for the East India Company. He chose a reliable gentleman to bring them home. A Mr Enberg.'

'I had a letter from Mr Enberg.'

'How extremely thoughtful of him. I liked him amazingly.'

'It would have saved a deal of worry and bother if you had let us know what was afoot. Your stepmother had no idea where you were, or whether you had received Mr Enberg's letter.'

'I am sorry if you were inconvenienced. I did not realize you were so interested in my niece and nephew's itinerary, or I would have informed you,' he said, in a lofty way he has, that might be only his innate arrogance coming through, or might be sarcastic.

'The children are also *my* niece and nephew,' I pointed out.

'Naturally I am interested in my own sister's children. What are they like?'

'Tolerably handsome. Ralph resembles his father, while Gwendolyn favors your family. Other than being a touch vaporish, she is a taking child. Ralph is quiet.'

'It is small wonder if she is vaporish, losing her parents, living in India, then having to cross the ocean with a total stranger.'

'Mr Enberg was chosen as he was *not* a stranger to them. His sister accompanied him, to play nanny. She was Lady Peter's good friend in India, and has been acting as the children's mother the past year. They were born in India – it is home to them. It is getting used to England that will take some doing. They'll settle in comfortably at the Manor. Ralph has already discovered the stables.'

More rational now, I finally grasped his meaning. He planned to keep the children himself. I was busy at once to alert him to my plan.

'Live *here*, in this little cottage?' he asked, astonished. 'There is not room to swing a cat. You could not possibly look after them properly – in a manner fitting their station, I mean.'

'The children of younger sons are not usually raised in a palace,' I pointed out.

'Particularly when the younger son made such a poor match,' he answered unhesitatingly.

'As to that, Peter had some money, which belongs to the children now. A larger house could be bought, or hired.'

'Peter had exactly ten thousand pounds as his portion. He would hardly have gone off to India, had he been wealthy. An annual income of five hundred would not go far to look after the children and your own household. I assume that was your meaning – to remove to this larger house paid for out of Ralph's income, with your mother and servants.'

'It would not make much sense to have two separate

establishments. We would pay our own way,' I answered hotly, recognizing the inference that I planned to live without expense in the setup.

'It would make even less sense to set up a new house for the children when I have several dozens of rooms standing idle. They will be raised by me, allowing the interest on the capital to compound, so that they have something substantial by the time they are fledged into the world. When the mother has no dowry to pass on to her daughter, you know, it adds the burden of trying to eke out something from the father's money.'

'But you don't want them! You admitted you consider them a nuisance.'

'You appear to consider them a bread ticket. I have a duty to my brother's family. I mean to execute it to the fullest extent.'

'Your duty is to see them happy and safe. They will be both with me – *us!* Mama too wants them.'

He allowed his head to turn slowly around the low-ceilinged, smallish sitting room, with the yellow furniture looking cheap in the full sunlight. 'What amenities can you offer, outside of your own company?' he asked bluntly. 'Englishmen in India live like kings. The children are accustomed to a good deal of waiting on. There will be nannies and governesses required, soon a tutor for Ralph, expensive schooling to provide. They will expect their mount each, and a groom.'

'They are only four and six. All these things are not required.'

'They soon will be. They have already suffered two violent upheavals in their short lives; first losing their parents, then leaving India, coming to a new country. It is my hope to see them permanently settled with me, to give them a feeling of security. They might be happy enough here for a year, two at the outside, at the end of which time another change of life style would be required. It is not necessary to subject them to so many stresses. Let them get used to living as they will always live. I can offer them the advantage of a fine home, a large circle of friends, teach them how to go on in society, offer them every advantage my position and wealth allow. It would be criminally selfish of you to try to restrict them to a genteel cottage, when they could have so much more.'

'Fine talking, Menrod! You have not *once* mentioned anything except material advantages. Orphans who have been buffeted around the world for a year now want *love*, and affection, someone who cares for their feelings. . . .'

He batted a langorous hand, dismissing my remarks as the ranting of a highly imaginative spinster. 'It is the manner in which I was raised, and their father, and all our friends. Servants provide that personal attention you speak of. They will not be alone when they scrape a knee or see frightening shadows in the dark. My decision has been taken.'

'Did Peter appoint you their guardian?' I asked.

'He died intestate. I told him to make those arrangements before he left England. Of course the children had not been born then. He failed to take my advice, and has landed me a messy kettle of fish.'

My dashed hopes revived immediately. 'You are premature to speak of having taken your decision, then. It will be for the courts to decide who will have the children. I mean to apply for custody.'

'Let us take our gloves off, ma'am,' he suggested, with a dangerous flash from his dark eyes. 'You think because your sister coaxed Peter to the altar, I am equally biddable. It is your intention to upgrade your free domicile to something more magnificent, with *me* footing the bills. No doubt you envision a London residence as well, or a seaside resort in Brighton for holidays. I am not such a flat. You won't get a penny out of me by these ruses. If the court is so blind as to turn the children over to your keeping, you will all stay here, with no help whatsoever from me. But they won't. I wish you luck in your endeavor.'

I was flattened by so many wrong charges. For full sixty seconds I sat like a witless woman, and when at last I could speak, I was hardly coherent. 'Don't think Hettie married Peter for his money. Much good it ever did her – dead before her time, and having to move to India with him. And don't think it is your money *I* want either. I wouldn't take a penny from you if I were starving. I want the children, and nothing else.'

'You might as well want the moon.' He arose languidly, to turn his attention once more in passing to the fire irons. He shook his head angrily. 'Will you be kind enough to convey my compliments to your mother, Miss Harris?' he said.

'When are we to see the children? Will you bring them today?' I asked.

'I will have them sent down immediately, if you like.'

'Send them for tea,' I said.

'Very well, but I want them home before dark.'

He bowed gracefully, and headed into the hallway. Fearful lest he direct his eyes to the left, toward the stairs, I ran after him, taking care to approach his right side. I could think of absolutely nothing to say, but he looked at me with curiosity, so I had to invent something. After all his ill-bred and outrageous charges, what I said was, 'I wish you will reconsider, about letting us have the children.'

It served the purpose. He was so upset, he marched straight out the door. 'Impossible. Good day.'

Pudge had enough sense to have the front door open for him. After it was closed, I ran to tell my mother the news. Like myself, she had grown weary from the long vigil, and gone up to her room. She probably knew Menrod was downstairs, but she is shy of him, or dislikes him. He subjected her and Papa to a grueling interview at the time of Peter's marriage to Hettie.

She never told me what he said, but since that day, she walks a block to avoid even meeting him on the street. I knew how she felt. I had never met such a cold, ruthlessly determined man.

# Chapter Four

$\mathcal{M}$r Everett arrived at about three o'clock, not long after Menrod departed. He had been to the London house and learned the children had been brought home. I felt unpleasantly beholden to him, after the foolish errand I had sent him on. To begin payment, I invited him to take tea with us. I would much have preferred to have the children to myself, but some extraordinary civility was owing Mr Everett. There was also the matter of the box stairs to get straightened out with all haste. After thanking him profusely for all his efforts on my behalf, I turned to the more worrisome matter.

'Would you mind very much to have your carpenters hammer on those panels they were preparing, as soon as possible?' I asked.

'The lads will be here this evening to take care of it. It is all arranged. I want you to promise you will not peek. In fact, you and your mother must take a late dinner with me this evening, so you will not be subjected to the hammering.'

'I shan't mind the hammering,' I assured him.

'Don't refuse me this favor. My cooks have been stuffing pheasants and baking pies and making ready since dawn. I wrote my instructions from London. You cannot refuse.'

Indeed I could not. One makes a dreadful error to put

herself in debt to anyone. I was now obliged to take dinner with Mr Everett. The splendors of Oakdene were known to me only by word of mouth, except for the exterior. It was left to conjecture what interior could match the oriental minarets, the baroque domes, gothic windows, and classical columns holding up the Georgian pediments of the outside. Of more immediate concern was the surprise he was preparing during our absence.

'It must look *exactly* as it did before. Menrod has been here complaining that we replaced an old poker with a new. He will not want his stairs changed.'

'If he is a man of good taste, he will like what I have planned.'

'It is not – not the dragons and lotus flowers, Mr Everett? So charming as they would look at Oakdene, you must see they would not suit this old cottage.'

'I know you disliked them, though Skanner says the Prince Regent himself has something similar at Brighton.'

'Plain panels, stained very dark brown. That is what I want.'

'You shall have exactly what you want,' he promised, allowing me to breathe easier.

Mrs Pudge had exerted herself to put on a tea to please two small children. When Everett sneaked in for a look at the table, it pleased him too. It consisted mostly of sweets, with some cold ham and cheese for the adults. Her famous Chinese cake was twelve inches high, elaborately iced with whipped cream. She had made up trays of dainties, tiny tarts, gingerbreads, sweet biscuits, to be taken with lemonade and tea. It more closely resembled a child's birthday party than anything else. To further bribe Gwen, I brought down her mother's favorite doll from her childhood. It was a rag doll, made by Grandmama, and dressed in a more modern mode by myself, with a pretty pink gown and bonnet. I had added a coiffure of new yellow wool. As I had no brothers, Ralph had no gift, but I hoped a four-year-old child would not realize he was being slighted.

I prepared my own toilette as carefully as the dolls. My second best green sarsenet gown was embelllished with my best lace collar and my only cameo brooch – a twin of one Hettie had. I wanted to look attractive, to make them like me. The children's preference would not carry much weight in court, but if I could show Menrod the children loved me, his insensitive heart might be softened. My resolve to have them was not swayed by the material advantages the Manor offered. Their bodily needs would be more lavishly met, to be sure, but I was far from being convinced catering to their every whim and withholding affection was the best method of rearing children. Only look at the results it had created in their uncle.

When all was ready, we sat awaiting the arrival of the guests of honor. Mr Everett regaled Mama and myself with details of his trip to London, and the various architectural wonders seen there. Pudge soon came stomping to the sitting room.

'They're here,' he said. You may try for a millennium to train a country couple to civil manners, but you will never succeed.

I flew up from my chair to welcome them in the hallway. The first sight that struck my eyes was the supercilious face of Menrod. Why on earth had he come? He said very distinctly he would 'send' them down. Soon my eyes sank lower, to see the children. They looked as described earlier, except for a pallor, no doubt the result of their loss and their fatiguing journey from India. They were shy. The girl held onto Menrod's fingers for dear life, while Ralph hid behind his legs, with only his dark head peeping out.

'Come now, children, remember your manners,' Menrod said gruffly, while physically pushing them forward. 'There is nothing to be afraid of. This is your Aunt Harris, your mama's sister. She won't eat you.'

The girl was the first to take a voluntary step toward me. She executed a wobbly curtsy, then ran back to Menrod. I felt the strongest instinct to grab them both into my arms, but suppressed it. My aim was to keep the mood low-keyed, friendly, but not overly emotional. While we stood smiling at each, Mama and Mr Everett came into the hall. There was a general confusion of introductions, along with some loud, ill-bred jollity from Mr Everett.

'So these are the little Indian orphans,' he said, sizing them up like a slab of lumber. 'I daresay it is the long haul that has made them so pale and frail. We will fatten them up in no time, eh, Miss Harris?'

Menrod lifted his slender brows in silent but quite obvious disapproval. 'I don't believe I am acquainted with your guest,' he said.

'This is Mr Everett, who went to London to meet the ship in case you did not,' I replied, then ushered everyone into the sitting room, past the disassembled stairway, which I was busy to block with my own body. Menrod's eyes roved all over the hall, for he was remarkably fond of this dismal little cottage, but soon they had settled on the new fire irons in the sitting room. While I made friends with the children, he took my mother to task about the ancient hardware. It was like drawing teeth to get a word from Ralph, but Gwen was more forthcoming.

'Uncle Menrod took us to see the white horses at Astley's Circus,' she told me, her great gray eyes as wide as saucers. 'He bought me a dolly, and he got Ralph a wooden rocking horse that he can sit on, only he falls off. My doll has glass eyes and real hair. She comes from France, so I call her Marie. Are you really my mother's sister?'

'Yes, I am. I expect she told you a great deal about me.'

'She told me you were young. I thought you would be a *girl*, not a lady,' she replied, disappointed. 'You don't look like Mama. She was very pretty.'

'There's a facer for you, Miss Harris,' Everett announced, chuckling loudly, and slapping his knee. 'Around these parts, Miss Harris is considered a rare beauty,' he added, seeing my displeasure at the interlude.

Menrod sat like a rock, finding no amusement in the conversation and adding nothing to it. Ralph was painfully shy. Hettie had called him boisterous, which made me realize how hard her death had hit him. He tried to clamber up on Menrod's knee, but was summarily put down, at which point he stood leaning against his uncle for security.

'I have something for you,' I told Gwen. 'Would you like to come upstairs and see your Mama's room, where she slept when she was a little girl, like you?'

'Yes, please,' she answered happily.

I wanted to get her alone, away from the others, to make a solid friend of her. I pointed out Hettie's bed, her clothespress, dresser, the window at which she used to sit, looking out on the rose garden. The rag doll was on the bed; it seemed a poor sort of a gift after Menrod's glass-eyed beauty, but I gave it to her anyway.

'Thank you,' she said, smiling. 'What is her name?'

I had no recollection what Hettie had called the doll, but invented the name Goldie, to match the golden wool recently added. The girl, though friendly, was not immensely taken with me. Her interest in her mother's room was polite rather than genuine.

'Shall we go and have our tea now?' she asked soon.

'By all means. Are you hungry?'

'No, we had a good luncheon, but I hoped there might be some sweets.'

The tea at least would be to her liking. Alas, it was not to Menrod's. He looked about the table for more substantial fare than Chinese cake and small tarts, finally settling for a single slice of ham and a pickle, which he picked at delicately. Ralph took one bite of a biscuit and two sips of lemonade. I don't recall that I ate anything at all, but Gwen and Mr Everett appreciated the party. Everett ate heartily, and was the major talker at the table as well.

He was one of those insensitive souls who believe the more loudly you shout at shy children, the more they are put at their ease, when anyone could see Ralph was petrified of his clamor and laughter. When he turned to me to whisper in a loud aside that the boy was as backward as a maiden, I gave him such a dark scowl he fell silent for full two minutes, before turning to tease Gwen about taking the last tart on the plate. 'That's right, eat it up. We don't want Miss Harris to have it, or she will be an old maid. That is what the ladies say, is it not, Miss Harris?'

Between Everett's bothersome racket, Menrod's looking down his nose at the food and the company, Mama's sitting as silent as a flower, and Mrs Pudge's slamming plates and cutlery around as though she were a mess sergeant, the meal was not at all pleasant. The real disappointment for me was that the children did not warm up to me. I felt sure that if I could get them alone, I could make long strides in securing their friendship.

To this end, I arranged to get Menrod aside for a moment after tea. Mama took the children into the garden. By intensive staring and head jerking behind Menrod's back, I transmitted to Everett that he was to accompany them. The only embarrassment in it was that he whispered in one of his carrying whispers, 'Do you want me to go along, Miss Harris? Is that why you are scowling at me?' I nodded vigorously.

He nodded back, winked, and said, 'I will be glad to oblige

you. I feared I had offended you, you were looking so oddly at me. What a dandy party it was. I ate so much cream cake I won't be able to do my own dinner justice. Don't forget you are to come to me this evening.'

Menrod had enough breeding to overlook the exchange. 'Alone at last,' he said ironically, after the others were out the door. 'I am highly curious to learn what you can have to say to me that may not be heard by the world.'

'I could not care less for the world's hearing me. It is only the children's ears I wish to avoid. It is about them, you see.'

'So I gathered. Are you quite easy in your mind now? Is there something you find amiss in them?'

'Not in them, but in your arrangements for their keeping. We have not settled where they are to be raised.'

'It is absolutely settled in *my* mind,' he replied, with a sharp glare from those frosty orbs.

'They are *my* relatives too. I want to have them.'

'You are knocking your head against a brick wall, Miss Harris. I have been at pains to engage their affection, so that they might feel easy with me. I can give them everything they require. You can offer nothing but such company as we have been submitted to here this day. Let us consider the matter closed. You will find me obliging in allowing you to have free access to them, for visiting.'

'*Allowing* me to *visit* them! Kind of you indeed! If I do exactly as you demand, no doubt you will allow me to call myself their aunt as well, and my sister their mother. You are in no position to be *allowing* anything. I have as much right to them as you. More.'

'More?' he asked, with a questioning look.

'Yes, more. They would be everything to me, my sole concern. To you, they are no more than a diversion. You will dash off and forget them as soon as the novelty of playing father has worn off.'

'I am not *playing* father. I *am* their guardian, and uncle. As to their being *everything* to you, I find that an extremely unhealthy statement. I don't want them smothered with love, growing up a pair of spoiled brats. Another woman's children should *not* be everything to you. If you feel the need of someone to mother, I suggest you follow the more normal course and get married, preferably *not* to the person who has been battering our ears the past hour with his raucous noise. It is incomprehensible to me that you chose to have him present at this first meeting with your relatives.'

He arose on this bold speech, sniffed, and began a disdainful bow.

'We are not finished yet. I don't mean to let the matter rest here.'

Mr Everett decided to return. He had been peeping in at the window, and saw my consternation. 'Is there anything I can do to help you, Miss Harris?' he asked, with a quick, questioning look at Menrod.

'Nothing, thank you, Mr Everett. I can handle this myself.'

'If you are sure, then I had best be getting back to Oakdene. I want to oversee preparations for our party. I shall come back and pick you and your mother up around seven-thirty, if that suits you.'

'That is fine. We'll be ready. Good day.'

Menrod and Everett nodded, neither saying a word about being pleased to have met, nor expressing any desire to continue the acquaintance. No sooner had we got rid of him than Mama returned with the children, making it impossible to continue the battle. Ralph attached himself to his uncle like a limpet, while Gwen began yawning and asking when they were to go home.

'Right away,' he told her. 'Shall I return tomorrow, Miss

Harris? I know you will agree this is not the optimum moment to continue our discussion. Shall we say, ten in the morning? I have an appointment in Reading at eleven, so will be passing by.'

'Excellent. I would not want you to go out of your way.'

'Thank your grandmother for the party, children,' he ordered.

Gwen thanked us on both their behalfs, then remembered to thank me for the doll.

'She didn't give *me* nothing,' Ralph was heard to say as they left, the first unsolicited statement to leave his mouth.

'Anything, Ralph,' his uncle told him, correcting his grammar but not his manners.

'That was very pleasant,' Mama said, with a sigh of relief. 'I am happy to see Menrod means to share them with us. It will be nice to see Hettie's children once a week or so. Gwen is very like Hettie at the same age. You would not remember, Gwendolyn, but Hettie had that same engaging manner. A pity little Ralph makes so strange, but we will win him over.'

Mrs Pudge came to the doorway, folded her hands on top of her white apron, and scowled. 'They liked the Chinese cake very well,' she congratulated herself. 'It is nearly gone.'

It was our cue for more strenuous praise of her cooking, followed by her reciting the many difficulties that had littered her path in its execution – the cream refusing to whip, the almonds not taking to blanching with any ease, the stove smoking and burning the first batch of tarts. I hardly listened; I was too distraught, thinking of reasons to proffer why the children should come to Lady Anne's cottage.

'Why is Menrod returning tomorrow?' Mama asked.

'To talk about the children staying with us,' I answered.

'They are so happy with him, I believe you ought to give up on that scheme,' she answered reasonably.

'You know he is never home two days in a row. They will be terribly neglected. Would you not like to have Gwen with us, the very picture of her mama?' I tempted.

'I *am* fond of Gwen, but I am not at all sure Ralph would be . . . He is very like Peter, is he not?'

'Peter was not so shy.'

'No, but he was hard to please, like Ralph,' she said, making her remark clearer.

'Will you be wanting any dinner at all, or was the tea enough to suit you?' Mrs Pudge asked.

'We are dining out,' Mama told her. 'Did Gwendolyn not tell you? I confess I forgot all about it myself, such a busy day as we have had.'

'Where are you going?' Mrs Pudge demanded.

'Mr Everett has invited us to dine at Oakdene,' Mama replied.

The hands that were crossed over Mrs Pudge's apron fell straight down and clamped on to her beefy thighs. 'You never mean it!' she exclaimed, her eyes large with distress. 'You're not going to sit down at that man's table.'

'We do not plan to dine standing up,' I answered sharply, from sheer ill humor.

'You fill all our faces with shame for you,' Mrs Pudge said angrily. 'That man is laying snares to entrap you into marriage, my fine lady.'

'Mr Everett is very comfortable to be with,' Mama said, smiling bemusedly. 'An excellent parti too, so very obliging of him to have gone all the way to London for us, and now he is to fix the stairs.'

'He is to make them back exactly as they were, and he had better do it,' I said, still vexed.

Mrs Pudge shook her head at my straying. 'So you won't be wanting any dinner, then?'

'Not tonight,' Mama confirmed.

Our housekeeper trudged at a weary gait from the door, soon to be heard in the hall telling her husband we had both run mad and were going to visit the heathen, who had thrown up a Babylonian tent at Oakdene.

# Chapter Five

Where does one begin to relate the wonders of an Oakdene? We were admitted to a house full of blinding light. From every table and wall, lamps blazed, illuminating such a host of finery as was never before assembled in one spot, unless it should be the garish residence of our Prince Regent. My first impression of Everett's saloon was the yards of red velvet draperies, held back by fringed gold satin cords. The ceilings were festooned with not only plaster moldings and large plaster medallions, but, painted on the flat spaces between, with Grecian deities and cavorting animals. The walls were covered with Chinese paper, the furnishings were mahogany trimmed with brass, while the upholstered pieces were covered in red and green. The yards and yards of floor were covered with carpets, all gaily patterned in red, blue and gold.

'My, how elegant! How colorful!' Mama exclaimed.

'I see no reason a house ought to be a dismal place,' he answered, pleased with the reaction.

'No one could call this dismal,' I said, my voice small, overwhelmed.

'I knew you would like it,' he answered, squeezing my elbow and directing my startled gaze to the three fireplaces that marched down the far wall. Two of them were of red marble, the central one green. All were flanked by caryatids, painted in life tones. Those ladies guarding the red fireplaces were outfitted in green, the ones guarding the green, in red.

I could go on and on – every table held a dozen intricate bibelots. There were silver bowls, crystal candle holders, vases of flowers, dishes of bonbons and nuts, small statuary, snuffboxes. Each room in the house, at least the dozen or so we saw downstairs, was equally elaborate.

After being given our choice of any wine in the world, we were told we would want champagne for this grand occasion. 'What occasion is that, Mr Everett?' Mama asked. She liked the place, but bewilderment had set in at such a surfeit of finery.

'Why, your first visit, to be sure,' he replied.

We ate our way through a dinner that would have filled a whole battalion of dragoons. Every meat and every delicacy known to Western civilization was on the board. The board was plenty large enough to hold them all. It cost him only ten guineas, due to his connections in the lumber business, and having it hauled free from London by a tranter indebted to him. We all sat at one end of this monumental table, each with a footman behind us, whose function was to dart down the table's length; retrieving tasty morsels to tempt us.

'Pass Miss Harris the prawns, lad,' he would say, then, before I had got a prawn on my plate, the footman would be ordered to look sharp, and bring me the asparagus, the butter boat, the broccoli, the peas, and where was the ragout, eh?

'You quite throw our simple party into the shade, sir,' I mentioned between servings.

'Don't apologize. An excellent sort of a do, in its own way,' he said leniently.

'I won't be able to eat for a week,' Mama said, refusing the smoked salmon.

'I do not eat so well every night,' he admitted, then went on to outline what his normal meal could consist of – no more than a dozen varieties of dishes, with no dessert, as often as not. 'No, I tell a lie. I always have a fresh fruit to top off on.'

The fact of this evening's being a special occasion was raised more often than our maiden visit to his home could account for. I began to dread the matter of my moving into Oakdene would come up before I got safely home. I was not mistaken.

After our Bacchanalia of champagne and dinner, Mama was invited by the host to take a tour of the kitchen and pantries. I assumed I too was to go along, but was restrained from following the housekeeper by a crippling grip on my elbow.

'I have something I want you to see in the saloon,' he said archly.

'I have not seen half the objects there,' I said. 'I caught a glimpse of a lovely painting, behind a statue by the green fireplace. A Canaletto, I think.'

'No, it is a genuine Italian thing,' he assured me gravely. 'I bought them all from a reputable dealer in London. But it is not the paintings I want to show you.'

As he spoke, he drew a box from a silver bowl that rested on a table. It was white velvet outside, in that telltale shape of a ring box. I knew my moment of exquisite misery had come.

My eyes were assailed by a diamond large enough to wear out a finger. The double row of sapphires and rubies that encircled the diamond would fatigue the whole hand. He drew it from its satin nest and lifted my left hand, trying to put it on the proper finger.

'No, really, Mr Everett, I cannot accept this.'

'You don't have to consider it an engagement ring. No strings attached, though you know by now what my intentions are where you are concerned, Gwendolyn.'

'I could not take it without being engaged,' I answered, aghast.

'Suit yourself,' he answered merrily. 'I won't cast a rub in your way if you care to consider yourself the future mistress of Oakdene.'

I am sure I behaved very badly, but at least I felt no desire to laugh, and it was truly a laughably enormous pledge of his troth. We pushed the ring back and forth between us, he insisting I accept it, even if I were not yet ready to accept him into the bargain, and I insisting I could not possibly do anything of the sort. I was very much aware of the debt of gratitude I owed him – for the trip to London, the box stairs, and a dozen other unwanted gifts of fruit and flowers he had delivered to Lady Anne's cottage over the past year or so. He was so kind, so generous, so good-natured, I felt a veritable vixen to have to tell him at last that I had no intention of getting married at all, to anyone.

He took it all in stride. 'Have another look around you,' he invited. 'You won't do better than Oakdene,' he tempted, as though it were a house I would be marrying, and not a man. 'I'll try you again a few weeks from now,' he warned, finally returning the ring to its box, and the box to its silver bowl. 'You'll find me a dogged salesman. I don't give up on one refusal. Many is the deal has taken me more than one or two tries to pull off. I didn't get where I am by being thin-skinned. Would it be an emerald you'd prefer?' he asked. 'They had a dandy one at Rundell and Bridges – cost a trifle more than the diamond, but you will never find me a skint.'

'No, no. The ring is beautiful.'

'If it is the wee ones you are worrying about, never give it a thought. We'll have a few of the chambers abovestairs painted pink and blue for them. We'll never know they are in the house. They won't bother us in the least.'

It was precisely the way they would be raised at Menrod Manor, and precisely what I hoped to avoid. 'The children are not a bother to me. I love children.'

'I'm fond of them myself.'

When Mama returned, Mr Everett showed us some plans he was drawing up for a Chinese pagoda that was to serve the job of belvedere in one of his gardens, at a cost of £1,265. Mama said it was beautiful, very handsome indeed, and I assured him it would be a fitting additon to Oakdene. This done, we were returned to Lady Anne's cottage, to view the new box stairs.

'Why don't you come inside with us, and see the job?' I asked when he began to re-enter the carriage.

'I'll be along tomorrow morning,' he answered.

It was unusual in the extreme for him to refuse any offer to enter our cottage. I sensed a skittishness in his manner, and chalked it up to disappointment at my refusing his offer. Just because he did not show his feelings was no indication he was less sensitive than others. I really felt badly about Mr Everett, till I went into the hallway and saw what he had done to our stairs.

He could not overcome his bent for finery. Despite his promises, he had sent the carpenters up to install a large brass railing, terminating in a dragon's head, with a ring hanging from it, like something used to tether horses. The spindles had been twisted into spirals, or perhaps what I stared at was snakes winding themselves around branches. It was perfectly hideous, and atrociously expensive. This was bad enough, clashing so dreadfully with the ancient timbers of the rest of the house, but there was worse. The whole side wall of the stair-case had been painted white, with gilt rosettes attached at random intervals to embellish the whole.

'How lovely!' Mama said. 'We are rid of the boxed-in walls at last, Gwendolyn. I shall run up the stairs this instant.'

She did as she said, to return a moment later praising the feeling of airiness, the freedom and ease of vision that had been gained by the change.

'Menrod will kill us,' I moaned.

'He's going to put a red carpet-runner down the stairs tomorrow,' Pudge said. He and his wife made free with us. If I did not
mention it, the Pudges were there with us. 'The lads didn't have
time to do it tonight. It took them forever to get the metal
bannister installed.'

'There was enough noise to give you the megrims,' Mrs
Pudge added in tones of pique.

Without hearing a single blow of hammer, I found my head
throbbing most painfully. Menrod was coming at ten o'clock in
the morning. There was no way this monstrosity could be
undone in time to keep it from him.

'Get the fire screen from the sitting room and cover up this
thing at once,' I said weakly.

'Cover it up? It is the only decent corner of the house,'
Mama objected.

In an extravagant, modern style, the stairs might have done
well enough in an hotel. In our humble, small, dark cottage,
they stood out like a diamond tiara on a scarecrow. The red
carpet would be the coup de grâce.

I arranged the fire screen at an angle that hid as much as
possible of the job from anyone entering at the front doorway,
as Menrod would be doing in eleven hours. I had a fairly sleep-
less night, comparing the efficacy of painting the whole with a
dark brown paint, versus moving large clothespresses into a
hallway scarcely wide enough to allow two people to pass. In
the end, I took the decision to send a note to Menrod Manor
very early, canceling the meeting. I disliked to have to ask
Everett to undo his job, but if I did not, Menrod would surely do
it for me, in a much less gracious way.

By morning, I had changed my mind. I went outdoors and
came in at the front door myself, looking to see how visible the
job was. If Menrod could be distracted as he entered, I felt the
fire screen would do well enough. It had to be placed at a ludi-

crous angle, jutting into the debouchement of the stairs, in order to cover the bannister, but there was nothing else for it.

All my scheming and worrying were in vain. He entered by the side door, as he happened to catch a view of me watering my plants in the conservatory on his way to the stable. He was about ten minutes early, which accounted for my not being waiting in the hall, to distract his attention.

'How very charming,' he said, casting a quick glance over my miniature jungle. 'This little conservatory is the only change that has been made to the cottage since its being built in 1600. It was added by a plant-loving ancestor in 1750. She was crippled, which accounts for its being attached to the house rather than freestanding, in the normal way. You have probably noticed there is a wider-than-usual doorway, to allow her Bath chair to be pushed in.'

'I have often wondered what accounts for the generosity of that doorway,' I replied, breathing a sigh of relief that he had entered this way. My relief soon turned to apprehension. Unless I could hold him here for the entire visit, he would have a completely unhampered view of the stairs when we passed through to the sitting room. My camouflage was arranged to impede the view from the front door only.

'It is actually balmy in here,' he went on. 'Such a pleasant change.'

'Why do we not sit down and have our discussion here?' I invited at once. 'Those rattan chairs by the window squeak abominably when first occupied, but are comfortable.' Without waiting for his answer, I took the three steps that put me at the chairs, and occupied one of them.

'How are the children today?' I asked.

'Gwen is suffering from an overindulgence in Chinese cake; Ralph is fine. Too many sweets are not good for them.'

'I agree. It was only for their first visit they were so indulged.

We do not habitually dine on cakes and tarts. I want to discuss with you again this business of guardianship of the children. I thought. . . .'

With a weary sigh, he raised a hand to stop me, much as Mr Everett does, except that his hand was more carefully manicured. 'Let us get this settled once for all. The children will make their home with me. You live only two miles away. You may see them any time you wish, either here or at the Manor, with the exception, of course, of those hours when they are at classes. You will have all the advantage of their company, without the inconvenience and expense of having them at the cottage to live.'

'They will be at classes for the better part of the day – Gwen, at least, and Ralph the same in a few years. They can hardly come down to us for an evening visit. That curtails their company rather severely.'

'Surely you do not plan to deprive them of an education?' he asked, with a startled stare. 'They would be at classes either here or at home. What is the difference?'

'The difference is that I planned to teach them myself.'

'You have mastered Latin and Greek, have you?' he asked ironically. 'Higher mathematics, history, French. . . . An amazing accomplishment, when one considers your sister was as ignorant as a swan.'

'Hettie was no more ignorant than any other lady of her class. Gwen will not be a student of Latin and Greek, unless you plan to turn her into a blue philosopher, some sort of intellectual freak,' I answered hotly.

'I do not consider accomplishments freakish, in either a lady or a gentleman. I have a theory that ladies can profit from higher learning quite as well as men. Their education is sadly neglected. A smattering of literature, a daub of poorly-pronounced French, water colors, and stitchery. That is poor preparation for life.'

'Nearly as poor as Latin and Greek, for a lady who will live out her life in England.'

'You know my views in this matter – the larger matter of where they will live. I can offer them everything; you – practically nothing. You mentioned taking it to the courts. Save your time and money. You'll catch cold at that. You will gain nothing but my ill will. One hesitates to throw his charity in the face of its recipients, but you are of course aware who provides this home in which you live.'

'This dismal, mouse-infested, dark, and draughty cottage in which we live is well paid for at ten guineas a year,' I answered, with more anger than common sense.

'You would think otherwise if you tried to hire an alternative accommodation. It is a charming spot, every detail of the place authentic. You are outstandingly fortunate to have the privilege of living here.'

'A privilege we share with two dozen mice in the thatched roof.'

'The occupant has some responsibility too. It is possible to be rid of mice, by a judicious use of traps and poison.'

'Yes, or by a good dry slate or shingle roof.'

'Out of the question. The thatched roof is the making of the place. It would lose ninety percent of its charm if I changed the roof. Well, can we consider the matter resolved, then? I keep the children, you visit them when you wish, at your own convenience and their availability, giving due consideration to their studies.'

'The matter will not be resolved in this high-handed fashion, milord. That is an ultimatum, not a compromise. Outside of your wealth and social position, you have little enough to offer. By your own admission, you consider them a nuisance. You spend more than ninety-five percent of your time away from the Manor. They would be abandoned to servants.'

'Lady Menrod is always at home, at the Dower House. Naturally I shall hire governesses, tutors, whatever they require. As they grow older, they can accompany me on some of my trips. They might profit from a summer by the sea, at Brighton.'

'If you really want to do what is best for them, you would let them stay with Mama and myself, where they would be every hour of every day with family who love and care deeply for them.'

'Miss Harris, there is no "if" about it. I *do* plan to do my best for them. I can do better than abandon them, to use your hard word, to a crotchety spinster and a widow, who have never been beyond ten miles of home. You know nothing of the world. Your interests are confined to this neighborhood, your few friends such people as Mr Everett.'

'There is nothing wrong with Mr Everett. As we are getting right down to brass tacks, Menrod, shall we take a look at *your* friends? Much of the society at the Manor is not suitable for children to meet. The whole neighborhood knows you had Mr Kean and a bunch of actresses there last year. Women of that sort. . . .'

'They were employees, hired to entertain my guests.'

'Yes, your *male* guests, and there was more than theatrics going on, to judge by local gossip.'

'When you base your opinion on *gossip*, you make rational conversation difficult. *Facts* are what we are both interested in, I hope. You may be sure a gentleman never entertains his lady friends in the nursery, at any rate.'

'Leaving the actresses aside, and omitting what rakes and scoundrels you associate with beyond this neighborhood, we are still left with your mistress. Mrs Livingstone, I believe, is the woman's name?'

He turned a furious eye on me, his head jerking up, to allow him to look down his sliver of a nose at me. 'Have you something against Mrs Livingstone?' he asked.

'Yes, the fact that she is your mistress, an extremely loose woman. Of more interest is the light the alliance sheds on your own character, for I cannot think that even you would be so low as to take the children to her. When a man is so steeped in lechery he must provide himself with a fancy at hand for the few days a year he spends at home, it stands to reason he is equally well provided for in those places he spends most of his time. A string of women stabled like horses across the country must cause the most lax judge to open up his eyes.'

'Are you daring to question my character?' he demanded, jumping to his feet and bumping his head on a low-hanging pot of ivy.

'I am stating a well-known fact. If it impugns your character, you must not place the blame on *me*. You did not hesitate to call me a crotchety, insular, ignorant spinster. We shall see which impediment the judge considers more serious: *my* lack of knowing Latin and Greek, or *your* lack of morals.'

'You are extremely foolish to come to cuffs with me, Miss Harris. If you are serious about wanting custody of the children, you had better hire yourself the best lawyer you can afford, and be prepared to curtail your expenditures accordingly. They don't come cheap.'

One says the stupidest things in the heat of argument. I chanced to think of Mr Everett, who must surely have as much money as Menrod, and was much more eager to spend it. Though I would not take a penny from him, I used his name in vain, or implied it at least. 'You are not the only one wallowing in gold,' I said airily. 'I have wealthy friends who would be happy to help with the finances.'

'A lady who accepts gifts of money from a man is hardly in

a position to dredge up the word *mistress* as an insult against others,' he pointed out.

'Unless the man has offered her marriage,' I shot back unwisely.

'If you think for one minute I would let that commoner be father to Peter's children, you are insane,' he said. 'Good day.' He stepped out the door.

It had been an upsetting interview. With my nerves in tatters, I did not notice at first which door he was walking through. Not till he was actually into the hall did I recall the surprise awaiting him there. I heard an anguished howl, not unlike the squeal emitted by a stuck pig. It was Menrod, catching his first glimpse of the brass railing, the white paint, the gold rosettes.

'What have you done? What is this – *abhorrence*?' he demanded. His face looked like a death mask, save that the eyes were wide open.

The fire screen cut down on the light coming from the front of the house. He pushed it aside, to stand staring in horror at the work, while I swiftly considered whether to tell him it was a mistake that would be undone at once, or to claim purposeful authorship of the foul deed. My own mood was angry enough to consider the latter, but in the end I told the truth.

'There was a little mistake,' I said mildly.

'A little mistake? A *little mistake*? No, madam, there was a gross crime perpetrated against architecture, art, and history. I'll sue him. I know who is responsible for this heinous – *thing*. Not even you, with all your lack of taste, your yellow tables and chairs and your potted weeds, could have devised anything so ugly. This is the work of Everett. Don't trouble to deny it. I have seen Oakdene. I recognize his hand in this. How *dare* you despoil this gem of a cottage?'

Without another word, he stalked out the door, to encounter two men carrying in a bolt of red carpet for the stairs. He knocked it out of their hands, making some loud but indistinguishable sound of threat. Whatever he said, it had the effect of getting the red carpet back onto the cart that stood at the door.

Mama, who has the magical ability to disappear at times of turmoil, came tripping down the stairs. 'Was that Menrod?' she asked fearfully.

'It certainly was.'

'Did he see the stairs?'

'Yes, he saw them.'

'I suppose he doesn't care for them.'

'He spoke of suing Mr Everett.'

# Chapter Six

$\mathcal{M}$enrod did not carry out his threat to sue. Instead he went storming down to Oakdene to ring a peal over Mr Everett. That same day, the carpenters returned to remove the abhorrence. Mama, with tears in her eyes, asked if she might have the bannister and railings and gilt-trimmed panels for a souvenir, as they were bought and paid for (but not by us).

'They will be here, if Mr Everett finds a use for them at home,' I told the workers. No doubt they would end up on his attic staircase.

A piece of wood of the proper age and size was found hidden on some wall at the church. Menrod worked some trick to get it removed to the cottage, and boarded back up the stairs with it. Mama repined loud and long; I was happy the thing was done without resort to law. One legal case was enough to handle at a time. I did not draw back from the battle for custody of the children. It had become a feud, a battle of wills and wits between us. I was required to resort to an inferior lawyer, owing to my shortage of funds, as I naturally had no intention of dunning Mr Everett for help.

My man was named Mr Culligan. He had done work in London for ten years, which led me to hope he knew what he was about. He had a dingy office on a second story of a side street in Reading, to which I went with my mother. It had been necessary to talk her back into wanting the children. This was accomplished by their absence. Menrod did not bring them to see us again, nor did we take the drive up to the Manor during the dispute. Judicious repetitions of his wretched character were less effectual than the boarded-up stairs in gaining her support. She had taken such a fancy to the brass dragon that she was very much vexed to lose it. A man who would condemn her to a lifetime of dark stairs was obviously no fit guardian for Hettie's children.

Two days after Menrod's visit to the conservatory, we took the drive into Reading. Mr Culligan was a tall, extremely thin man with ginger-colored hair. He had a prominent nose, splotched with broken veins, and a narrow face. He wore an outdated jacket of some cheap blue material. His cuffs were frayed, his watch chain pinned to his waistcoat, his boots down at the heels, but he seemed capable enough despite these signs of poor business. Customers do not run to the door of any but local-born professionals in Reading. It would be his London sojourn that accounted for his scarcity of clients, but I knew Menrod would hire a top city man, and did not want a country bumpkin pitted against him.

I outlined the situation to him, making much of Gwendolyn being my name-child, and the closeness between her mother and myself. He asked me three times whether I was quite sure there was no will leaving the children in Menrod's guardianship; when I convinced him there was not, he wished to know whether there was something which might be considered a letter of intent, a letter from Lord Peter in which some intimation had been given that Menrod was to consider himself their custodian. Knowing what a poor correspondent Peter was, and feeling it unlikely Menrod would have kept any chance missive that happened to imply anything of the sort, I told him no. He clucked and shook his ginger head, and finally advised me not to sue for custody.

'The courts will favor his lordship,' he said comprehensively. 'He is a man, a peer, in a position to do everything for them.'

'He is a lecher,' I declared, equally comprehensively.

His greenish eyes widened at this telling speech. 'Ah – a bad character. This is more like it,' he said, rubbing his hands together in glee. 'We will need some evidence,' he went on. 'Could you just give me some names and places of abode?'

I found myself reluctant to utter the name of Mrs Livingstone. Not that she is any great bosom bow of mine; I do not know the woman but to nod to her on the street, after having met her there so many times over the past few years, yet it seemed a hard thing to blacken her character. 'Any number of women in London,' I said, hoping to dismiss the evidence in this vague way.

'That'll cost us something, to go to London and have him followed. It is the client, that being yourself, Miss Harris, who will be paying rack and manger for either a hired snoop or myself.'

'Why, that is not necessary, Gwendolyn,' Mama objected. 'There is Mrs Livingstone living in state in that grand brick house on the river, not a mile away from here.'

I opened my mouth to shush her, but Culligan's hand was already flying across the page, while he mentioned it would be better still if we could give him another name or two. 'I don't know that *one* mistress would blacken his character, him being a bachelor, you see. It might be what you call an extenuating circumstance.'

'*Might* be?' I asked. 'Don't you know for sure? You are a lawyer.'

'Each case is unique. I have never had one just like this before. It is his lordship being a lord that clouds my under-standing. Not to say the law is different for the rich and titled, but if he managed to get a jury of his peers, you see, they would certainly see nothing amiss in a bachelor having a fancy. They would think him a rum touch if he had not. If you could tell me something in his background that is *really* wicked, we would have a stronger case. You wouldn't happen to know if he molests children – that would be an excellent point. Or we could use beating his servants, insisting on having his way with the serving wenches – any sort of perversion in particular would be entirely helpful to us.'

'No! Good gracious, no! He is not a monster of depravity. He is only inconsiderate of the children's day-to-day comfort. I do not want you asking such questions as that of his friends.'

'I deal subtle-like,' he assured me.

I next mentioned Peter's inheritance of ten thousand pounds, which would provide them a more comfortable home than Lady Anne's cottage, lest Menrod use that against me.

'Aha!' Culligan said, his lips splitting in a smile. 'It is their blunt he's after. That is an excellent point. Would you happen to know if he's ever got money from anyone else by these underhanded means?'

'Certainly he has not! It is not the children's money he is after, either. That was not my meaning. Really, I think you are going at this the wrong way, Mr Culligan. I do not want Menrod traduced so wantonly as you are doing.' I was begin-ning to consider dropping the case entirely, or the lawyer, at least.

'Now I see you are vexed with me,' he said. 'You must not think because I speak very frankly to you within these walls that I will shout the same questions about the countryside, Miss Harris. Client privilege – what you say to me here will never be uttered by me outside. It is my duty, as your lawyer, to do my best to win the case for you. You may be sure Menrod is following the same course with his man, in having your character looked into. It is the normal way of going on. Law is a messy business, but we'll wrap the whole up in a clean linen when the time comes to go public. Don't take another pique, but I really must enquire whether there is anything in your own background that don't bear scrutiny. No liaisons, never run afoul of the law, paid your debts all up proper, and so on, have you?'

'My character is good,' I said, incensed, though I knew the question was necessary.

'We owe the greengrocer two pounds,' Mama reminded me.

This naive statement convinced Culligan we were a pair of angels. He went into a merry peal of laughter. It was a long, distasteful interview. I was told to go through my correspondence with Hettie, for I had kept her letters, and discover whether there was anything indicating I should be the children's guardian in case they were orphaned. I knew there was nothing of the sort, but he insisted I check.

I felt as though I had been rolling in a gutter when we finally got out into the clean sunshine. There was something depraved about the visit.

'You did not tell him about the stairs, Gwendolyn,' was my mother's first comment. 'That shows a bad streak in his character, to make Mr Everett take them out, when they were so much better than the old.'

'I fear that is a mark against us, rather than Menrod. We agreed not to change his house, and we broke our agreement. I will find those demmed old pokers and tongs this day, and restore them as well.'

'This is not the time to take up swearing, my dear, when that wretched man is having us investigated. We did not give our usual plum cake to the church bazaar last Christmas, either, when Mrs Pudge had the cold. That is bound to come up, and cause a scandal. But then, your papa was a minister of the church, the best man who ever drew breath. That will have some weight in our favor. Three livings – a very successful minister.'

Three livings was the very thing to turn the common folks against us, smacking of privilege and even of a grasping nature. Every minutia of our simple lives was put under scrutiny, the process continuing long after we got home.

'Are we to have control of the kiddies?' Mrs Pudge asked when we were admitted.

'I fear it will be a long process,' I told her. I was coming to see it would also be expensive. Culligan would wear a new shirt with unfrayed cuffs now, if he wished, and a proper chain and fob for his watch too.

'Never worry about it, Miss Gwendolyn,' she said, taking pity on me in my affliction. 'I have been looking it up in my psalter, given to me by your dear papa, and have found succor. The wicked man, in his pride, may persecute the poor – aye, boast of his heart's desire to get hold of our children, but he'll never do it. God that sits in His heaven won't allow it. He shall laugh at the ungodly. Our Gwen and Ralph will be laying their dear little heads to rest here before you can bat an eye.'

'I hope so, Mrs Pudge.'

'I'll bring you both a cup of tea this very instant. You look as worn out as a pair of old shoes. I would have had it ready for you, but that old devil cat of Menrod's has been chasing my Lady again, the bounder. Something is wrong with the world when I have to keep her locked inside the house to preserve her from the scoundrel. Speaking of which, Mr Everett was here. He left you off a note.'

She brought the note with the tea. Both were delightful. The note informed us that Menrod was seen passing Oakdene in his traveling carriage, obviously en route to London. Some fine-honed questioning in town had confirmed this suspicion, which he knew would be good news for us. He added that the children were not with him.

I sat right down at my desk and wrote to Culligan, telling him that already Menrod had abandoned the children. When Pudge returned from delivering the note for us, he had a reply from Culligan, a letter containing such an outrageous and brilliant idea that my opinion of the man rose higher. It was couched in confusing legal jargon, as so many of his speeches were, but the gist of it was that I should kidnap the children, bring them to Lady Anne's cottage, while I had the chance. He assured me I would be immune from legal action, as Menrod had no more real right to them than I. Till custody had been granted by the court, the children were in fact wardens of the court. In a prosaic vein, he added that possession was nine points of the law, though he could find no actual precedent in his books for this common knowledge.

Mama was extremely doubtful about the wisdom of this course, but when both Mrs Pudge and her husband lauded it, she was talked around.

'Didn't the good Lord send an archangel to lead the baby Jesus away from Herod?' Mrs Pudge demanded of Mama. There was no denying such an oft-told tale. 'Miss Gwendolyn will lead those innocent babes of Miss Hettie's home to safety too. We'll have all the heathen in derision by the time he gets back, with the doors barred,' she added, causing some little doubt as to who were the heathens in the case.

To tell the truth, I felt as guilty as one when I drove up to Menrod Manor and presented myself to the butler under the pretext of taking Gwen and Ralph for a drive.

'Lord Menrod did not *forbid* it, I trust?' I asked, with a smile. 'He assured me I might see them as often as I wished. He would not have hired a governess yet, I assume, so they will not be at their books.'

'Oh, no, Miss Harris, not yet. He has gone up to London for the purpose,' the butler told me.

'Did he say how long he would be gone?'

'He will return as soon as his business is complete – a few days, he mentioned.'

'Who is looking after the children in the meanwhile?'

'Mrs Butte, the housekeeper, has them in her charge. They are with some of the servant girls at the moment, having a game of skittles.'

The children were not so happy as one could have wished to be taken away from their game. 'Good afternoon, Aunt,' Gwen said. Ralph said nothing. He crossed his ankles and stuck his thumb into his mouth, a trick I had not noticed before. I told him to remove it and get his jacket to come with me for a drive.

'Where are we going?' Gwen asked.

'To visit your grandma,' I answered.

'Does she have some cakes today?'

'Of course she has. If you are very good, we shall give you some.'

The bribe got them out the door without resorting to violence, though Gwen had the poor manners to mention twice more that she was enjoying the game of skittles very much, and winning too.

They were made as welcome as the prodigal son at the cottage, where Mama and Pudge awaited their arrival. Mrs Pudge was even then laboring over a plum cake to please them.

'May we have the cake now?' Gwen asked, when she had been seated for two minutes.

'It is only three o'clock,' I pointed out.

'You said we could have some, Aunt,' she reminded me.

Ralph stuck his thumb in his mouth and rested his head on the upholstered arm of the chair he sat in. 'That is no way for a little gentleman to behave in company,' I told him.

'Ralph is hungry,' his sister told me, wearing a sly little smile. Hettie had used to have a very similar expression, which had faded from my memory over the years. Nature is kind; she lets us hold onto what is dear, and fades the less beguiling memories.

'Then Ralph shall have an apple,' I answered.

'Uncle Menrod lets us have cake,' she answered.

'Does he give you sweets whenever you want them?' I asked, thinking I might have a bit of poor rearing practice here for Culligan to use. A despicable trick, I know, but this was war.

'No, he doesn't,' Ralph said dismally. 'He makes us eat gruel for breakfast, and beefsteak for lunch. It will make us strong.'

'Can we play skittles till teatime?' was Gwen's next speech.

'We do not have any skittles, dear. Would you like to look at some books instead?' I asked.

'I don't like books. Have you got any more of Mama's dolls?'

'No, I gave you her only doll. Do you like to draw?'

This proved acceptable. For full five minutes she sat and drew, insisting at every stroke of the pen that we all gather and admire her squiggles. The child was deplorably spoiled; she required a firm hand, and I had one ready and willing to trim her into line, but first I must cozzen her along by more pleasant manners. After ten minutes, Mama had the inspired idea of sending her to the kitchen to help Mrs Pudge make the cake. I breathed a sigh of relief to see the back of her, tossing her curls as she hastened out.

My interest then turned to Ralph. 'Can I go to the stables?' he asked timidly.

'Let us wait till after tea.'

'After tea we will be going home.'

'Not immediately after tea. Would you like to stay here tonight, Ralph?' Mama asked.

He considered this a while. 'No, thank you, Grandma,' he answered, but not in his sister's saucy way. 'I am learning to ride the wooden horse Uncle Menrod got me. I will go home and ride it after tea. Uncle says when I learn to ride like a proper cavalier, he will get me a real pony.'

'Not for a few years, I hope!' Mama exclaimed.

'Papa was riding when he was four.'

'That is much too young. It is dangerous,' she told him, her cheeks blanching.

'*I* am not afraid. I am not afraid of anything. Except the dark, and the water. Mama and Papa were killed in the water,' he told us, his eyes shining with fear.

I felt it best to divert his thoughts, and offered to read him a story. We went together upstairs to the small room where our childhood relics were stored. There being only two girls in the family, we had not those tomes most likely to appeal to a young boy, but he found a book of old English tales having to do with knights on chargers and ladies locked in towers, that appealed to him. He sat very close to me, actually clutching onto my skirts. I felt a rush of tenderness for him that was sorely lacking toward his sister, though I had always assumed it would be the girl, my own name-child, who would appeal more to me.

'Would you like to sit on my lap, Ralph?' I asked.

'Yes, please,' he said, easing himself up and leaning his little dark head against my chest. His fingers played nervously with the folds of my skirt. He felt such a pitiful, bereft little soul that I wanted to just cradle him in my arms and comfort him. There was a lump in my throat that made reading difficult. This child, whatever about this sister, needed more than a house-keeper and an uncle who bought him a wooden horse, then drove off in his carriage to let the boy sit alone, learning to ride it.

We got on famously, Ralph and I. By teatime, he was clinging to me quite as fiercely as he used to cling to Menrod. Gwen,
happy to have a large cake before her, became communicative
and friendly, easy to like. Mama smiled dotingly on her, occasionally wiping away a tear. Gwen thanked us politely when tea
was over, and said it was time she be getting home. It galled
me, to hear the children call Menrod Manor home.

'As your uncle has gone to London for a few days, we
thought you might like to stay here with us,' I said, giving a
casual sound to it. Letting them know a battle was raging over
them was the last thing I wanted.

'*I* would like to stay,' Ralph said at once.

Gwen sat considering the invitation carefully. I had an intu-
ition her mind grappled with the probable quantities of cake
and attention the two homes afforded. 'All right, we'll stay,' she
decided. Her next speech showed me I was too hard on her.
'Will you show me my mother's room again, Aunt? May I sleep
in her bed?'

She received a sympathetic yes to both questions, and a
more sincere smile than usual from her aunt as well. 'I shall
send a note up to the Manor, asking them to send down some
clothing,' I mentioned to Mama. I knew my eyes were sparkling
with triumph, could feel the smile curl my lips.

'Good girl,' Pudge congratulated as I went into the hallway
toward the study. He had been auditing the whole from his
hiding place outside the door. I dashed off a polite note, and
had Pudge take it up to the Manor. He was back within the
hour, to tell me Mrs Butte thought it would be better if the children returned at once to the Manor. Within five minutes more,
one of Menrod's lesser vehicles was at the door to collect them.

'My niece and nephew are remaining with their grandmother
for the present. You may tell Mrs Butte so, as she will want to

inform his lordship when he returns. Good night.'

'Yes, Miss Harris,' the servant answered respectfully. All Menrod's servants are well behaved, but there was an expression of startled incredulity on the young man's face at my daring.

# Chapter Seven

We had two uninterrupted days of Gwen and Ralph's company. It was long enough to convince me Gwen was a sly, self-willed girl, possessed of a wide streak of charm, which she could turn on at will to get her own way. Any wish we had to deny her was met with the statement that Uncle Menrod let her do it, or have it, depending on the situation. You would no sooner be convinced she was a selfish, conning rogue than she would show some uncommon concern and understanding for her brother, or Grandma, or even Aunt Harris. Her understanding was quick, her conversation entertaining for a child her age. Mama said at least a dozen times a day she was 'so very like Hettie.' I confess shamelessly I fell in love with Ralph. Nothing pulls at the heartstrings so violently as a shy little child who attaches himself to you and shows openly he would rather be with you than anyone else in the world. It was Ralph's way with me. Whether I was in my conservatory tending the plants, in the study going over accounts, by the fireside sewing, or bustling about the house helping Mrs Pudge, he was there. He only left my side to go to the stables for half an hour each morning and afternoon. On his last visit he returned earlier, as he had skinned his finger. I gave him a large plaster, to make him feel important.

It was these trips to the stables that brought to a head the matter of clothing. Mrs Butte did not send any down from the

Manor. Gwen, though neat as a pin, had got cocoa spilled on her gown, while Ralph was grimed from helping the groom. On the evening of their first whole day with us, we women got our heads together to see what was to be done. We decided to make Gwen a new robe, cut down from one of Hettie's, while Ralph was to be reoutfitted in a shirt and trousers cut down from an old outfit of my father's. The measuring and cutting were done that evening, the sewing the next day. Shortly after lunch, they had their clean clothing on, while their better outfits were being cleaned. We were not so ambitious as to tackle a jacket for Ralph. There is some mystery involved in setting in a sleeve, that has evaded the three of us during our whole lives. The third was Mrs Pudge. Any attempt results in an unsightly puff at the sleeve's top, just where it joins the shoulder. This is well enough in a lady's gown, but would not do for a boy's jacket.

Mama took care of Gwen's dress, fashioning it in a manner similar to the pinafores my sister and I had worn some twenty years ago. She could not resist the impulse to add Hettie's childhood coiffure to cap her effort. Gwen's curls were done up in a topknot no longer seen in England, though it looked very sweet. Gwen had been at pains to bring Mrs Pudge, the provider of sweets, around her thumb. As we took dinner that evening, another of the foot-high Chinese cakes was on the table. With our shortage of servants and space, the children dined with us, as is done in smaller households. At the Manor, they would be upstairs, eating with servants.

'May I have some tea?' Gwen inquired politely.

Our limited supply of lemons had run out that afternoon. We had not been prepared for so much lemonade as was drunk by the children. 'Why not? I'll make it half milk,' I agreed.

Ralph too had to have tea then, more for the attention than any real desire to drink it. He spooned an unconscionable quantity of sugar into his cup, but as it was clear he was not going to drink it, we did not worry.

We were just terminating a very enjoyable meal when there was a loud knock at the cottage door. Mrs Pudge, loitering near the dining room door, said, 'I'll get it. Pudge is washing my pots in the kitchen.' She went absentmindedly, holding a serving bowl of carrots in her hand, to do so. As we had not seen Mr Everett for two days, I had a feeling it would be he, though the hour was inconvenient.

Within seconds, Mrs Pudge came trotting back to inform us, 'He is in a great pucker, come to pick up the kiddies.'

'Menrod?' Mama enquired, quite unnecessarily.

Mrs Pudge nodded her topknot. 'He's looking over them stairs with a magnifying glass.'

This was an exaggeration, though he was actually sticking his fingers into the grooves where one piece of wood met another. 'There is no matching the original work,' was his gruff greeting. 'This is poorly done. I'll send my carpenter down from the Manor to see what he can do.'

'Good evening,' I said. 'Our housekeeper tells me you are come to see the children. They are just finishing dinner. Would you care to wait in the sitting room? We shall be finished presently.'

'I would not dream of disturbing your dinner. I shall join you there,' he answered, leveling a menacing stare at me.

He followed closely at my heels, making me minutely aware of how casually we were dining, by his black evening suit. He must have taken dinner all alone too, or more likely would do so when he returned to the Manor, as we keep country hours. I knew nothing would be done in the country style there.

Mama received a proper bow before he turned his attention to the children. His eyes opened wider to see Gwen decked out like a fashion plate from the last century, shoveling large forkfuls of the cake into her mouth. She stopped to greet him. Ralph sat silent, playing with the bandage on his finger.

'Sit down, Menrod,' I invited. 'Mrs Pudge, perhaps our guest would like a glass of wine.'

'Thank you, no. I shall just wait till you have all finished dinner, then we must have a private talk.' His eyes flickered over the children, indicating his words were not for their ears. 'Your mother, you, and myself,' he added.

Mama, the coward, immediately set down her cup and said, 'Come along, children. Grandma will take you upstairs. You speak to Menrod, Gwendolyn. You know our position, and can discuss it with him.'

I was surprised Menrod said so little to the children. I thought he would be eager to ingratiate himself. He examined them closely enough, to be sure, but there was so grim a set to his jaws, that everyone was ill at ease. As Ralph got up, Menrod said, 'I see you have hurt yourself, Ralph. Was a doctor called?'

'A mere scratch,' I said.

'The size of that bandage would indicate a more serious accident,' he replied suspiciously. 'Come here, Ralph, and let me see if it has been properly cleaned. We don't want blood poisoning setting in.'

Ralph went dutifully. The bandage was removed, to show a scratch already well on the way to healing. 'Do you think he will live?' I asked satirically.

Menrod said nothing. We went to the sitting room, while Mama took the children upstairs. I indicated a chair for him by the cold grate. We do not ignite our logs unless it should be necessary, owing to the smoke that seeps slowly into the room. It is usually required to open a window, which undoes all the good of the fire. I took up the chair opposite, both of us sitting as stiffly erect as a pair of formal statues.

'May I know what you hope to accomplish by this stunt?' he

asked, reining in his temper.

'My aim was to enjoy the company of my niece and nephew, as you were not doing so. "Anytime I wish, either here or at the Manor, providing they are not busy with their classes," you said. You forgot to inform your housekeeper of the arrangement.'

'Cut line, Miss Harris. We both know that was not your ultimate aim. This amounts to nothing less than kidnapping.'

'You had best consult with your solicitor, sir. Kidnapping implies *illegal* removal of someone from his rightful guardian. I believe there is a matter of ransom involved as well. You are no more their rightful guardian than I am. The children are wards of the court, at the moment.'

He withdrew a sheet of paper from his pocket, a long sheet, plastered with impressive-looking red seals, several black signatures, and a deal of Latinate mumbo-jumbo. 'As of noon today, I am their legal guardian,' he said, passing the sheet rather quickly under my nose. I grabbed hold of a corner of it before he could withdraw it.

I scanned the sheet quickly, confirming that the piece of paper did indeed appoint him sole guardian, but on an interim basis only, till the case could be permanently decided by the courts. I was stunned at the speed with which he had moved, and out of reason cross that Culligan had not done the same on my behalf. They had told me at the Manor he went to London to hire a governess – an effort to put smoke in my eyes.

'Your people at the Manor were misinformed. I was told you went to London to hire a governess.'

'I did that too.'

I continued reading the sheet. Close to the bottom I discovered what I wished to know. His interim guardianship was for six weeks only, this apparently being the period necessary for him to gain permanent control. 'It was possible to find one willing to leave the city for only a six-week job, was it?' I asked.

'My servants are hired subject to a probationary period. If she works out, I shall keep her on.'

'Providing you still require her services. My solicitor feels my chances of gaining custody are good.'

'You took my advice? Whom did you hire?'

'A man from the city,' I answered grandly, and also vaguely.

'As you have not left the neighborhood, I must assume you refer to that muckracker of a Culligan, from Reading. I don't know of anyone else working locally who was run out of London.'

'I have employed Mr Culligan. He seems capable.'

'Capable of robbing you blind. If you are not involved in a worse legal battle than this for custody of the children before you are through, you may count yourself lucky. His last client – two or three years ago – ended up in Old Bailey on fraud charges. Beware what you put a signature to, in your dealings with him. He invents the crooked schemes, but is careful to arrange matters so that his clients bear the blame.'

'We cannot all afford to dash off to London to hire an expensive man from the city.'

'Very true. We cannot all afford to raise two children properly either. For what reason is Gwen dressed like a character from a medieval play? Do you want to make the child a laughing stock? I trust she has not been seen on the streets in that antique outfit?'

'She has not been on the streets at all. She has not left the house.'

'You have kept her cooped up here for over forty-eight hours, stuffing her with sweets and depriving her of fresh air and exercise. Handsomely done! I would have easy work gaining custody if I left them with you for a fortnight.'

'She wanted to stay in. Ralph was out – he went to the stables twice a day. And pray do not raise any foolish mention of that scratch on his finger.'

'My only interest in it is that you have made a big to do of nothing, putting a king-sized plaster on it. It is typical of the overmothering he would be subjected to here, with two ladies hovering over him like a pair of broody hens. He is half a girl already, owing to the way he was raised in India. He wants toughening up. He won't get it here, but he will damned well get it from me.'

'He is a sensitive boy – a *child*! How can you be so unfeeling?'

'Boys become overly sensitive when they are too much protected and too much with women.'

'If you bully him, Menrod. . . .'

'I am not a monster. I realize the peculiar circumstances he has been subjected to. I find it wantonly cruel of you to add to the turmoil by this game of playing mother, snatching the children away, and very likely filling their heads with stories against me.'

'I have not! We weren't talking about *you*! We have better things to discuss.'

'Those children are going to make their home with *me*. Make no mistake about that. If you turn them against me, you only make their role, and my own, more difficult, not that you care a groat for the latter. What *will* appeal to your selfishness is that you also lessen your chances of having any access whatsoever to them. If I continue to find your influence disruptive to their development, I shall get an injunction forbidding you within a country mile of them. It can be done. Don't doubt for an instant I will do it, if this nonsense continues.'

'You have a high opinion of your powers. Even lofty earls are not above the law. If the County Court decides in my favor, we shall see who is kept a mile from them.'

'The County Court is not involved. This will be settled in Chancery.'

'I don't care if I have to take it to the Supreme Court.'

'Chancery is an integral part of the Supreme Court. I can only assume you have had a hasty lesson in forensic matters from Mr Culligan. I should have thought *even* *he* would at least know where to apply for custody.'

'He knows plenty, including a few tricks your expensive solicitor doesn't.'

'You overestimate my expenditure. Sir Nathan Beckwith refused to accept any payment to represent me. He is considered the foremost expert in these custody battles. Well, see you in court, Miss Harris. Would you be kind enough to have my charges sent down now? It is past Ralph's bedtime.'

Every atom of my body wanted to strike out at him, to push him out the door and bar it, to hold onto the children, most particularly dear little Ralph. But he had the interim custody decree from Chancery, and rather than submit the children to any more fuss, I did as he asked. Mama brought them down.

'Do I *have* to go now?' Ralph asked, holding onto my fingers. 'I hoped you would read me another story, Aunt.'

'Another time, dear. Your uncle is taking you to his house tonight.'

'Your wooden horse is waiting for you at home. He is getting lonesome,' Menrod said, with an enthusiastic forced smile.

'Did you buy me anything in London?' Gwen asked.

'You might find a bag of sugarplums in your room,' he tempted.

'Tch, tch, stuffing the child with sweets!' I said.

'An occasional treat is permissible,' he informed me.

'When can we come back?' Ralph asked.

'We'll be back one of these days,' his uncle answered, revealing nothing.

The children were not totally desolate to leave, in light of the treats awaiting them at the Manor.

'So you let him walk off with Hettie's little kiddies, did you?' was Mrs Pudge's greeting when she strolled into the sitting room.

'He had been to London to get an interim custody decree arranged. There was no preventing him.'

'Aye, the throne of iniquity frameth mischief by a law,' she answered sadly. 'The courts always take the counsel of the ungodly.'

'He sneaked off to London for the very purpose of arranging it quickly,' I explained.

'They got their heads together to commune of laying snares privily,' she declared.

'We must go to see Culligan tomorrow, Mama.'

'Yes, we must hear what he has to say about it.'

'Menrod has no good opinion of the man,' I said.

'A brutish man knoweth not, neither does a fool understand,' Mrs Pudge thought.

'He is not a fool, whatever about being a brute. I fear he will be hard on Ralph.'

'I meant your Culligan,' Mrs Pudge told me. 'If he wasn't a fool, he would have got a decree framed up, like Lord Menrod.'

'It is odd he did not think of it,' Mama said, frowning. 'It is Gwen I hate to see go. It was so very like having Hettie back in the house – not that you are not excellent company, Gwendolyn. You handle everything for me, but Hettie and I. . . . She was my first-born, you know, a piece carved out of my heart. You did not come along for five whole years, so she was good company for me while you were still in swaddling clothes.'

It was no secret that Hettie was my mother's favorite. It was tolerable to me, as I was equally favored by my father. Really we all four got on together. There was no rancor in our family. Hettie had more of her daughter's charm, in my view, and less of her self-interest, unless that fond deceiver, Time, leads me astray. Hettie *had* set her cap straight at Lord Peter, but I believe it was love that accounted for it, not a desire to wear a title.

I explained in detail about Menrod's decree. We discussed what was to be done, but as we were both as innocent as newborn babes in legal matters, our only decision was to return to Culligan on the morrow, which we did.

# Chapter Eight

$\mathcal{M}$r Culligan was not at all dismayed to learn Menrod had got interim custody of the children. 'There's many a slip twixt the cup and the lip,' he assured us. 'If he's the sort of man my investigations tell me he is, six weeks will turn the little ones sour on him. The girl, at least, is old enough to speak her mind.'

'It is the boy who is fonder of me,' I told him.

'I suppose he has the use of his tongue as well, at four years,' he pointed out. 'Not that much attention will be paid to such a bunting. I have been looking up precedents, in these tomes you see here on my desk, ladies. I am giving your case my entire attention. The situation is not desperate.' His hands reached out and touched the dusty volumes. His frayed cuffs had not yet been replaced. I hoped he meant to do so before he was required to appear in Chancery. As he had now one paying customer, I thought he would refurbish his toilette.

'It is not far from it. What do the books say?' Mama asked.

'The solution is really very simple.' He smiled cunningly. 'All you have to do, ladies, is find yourselves a husband – either one of you, but preferably the young lady. It should not be impossible.'

'Mr Everett!' Mama said at once, with a delighted smile. 'Why my daughter has just had a most excellent offer.'

'What has a husband to do with it?' I asked.

'It gives you your good, solid family unit. In these precedents I spoke of, I have found half a dozen cases where the kiddies went to the family that had two parents. A normal family unit, they call it. Stands to reason a child wants a mother and father. Yessir, if we cannot get anyone to testify in court that Lord Menrod is a villain, though there are any number will say so behind his back, then we'll hit him with a normal family unit. Did you take Everett up on his offer?'

'No, I did not.'

'Better snap him up fast, within the six weeks of the decree. Is he a man of means and good character?'

'Yes, but I do not mean to marry him.'

'He is a millionaire – lives in a mansion,' Mama felt it necessary to add.

'Indeed! Is it *that* Everett you speak of, the nabob from the city?' Culligan verified, greatly impressed. 'The one that built himself the mansion on the Reading road?'

'Yes, but I am not getting married, even to win the children,' I insisted.

'If you don't plan to take my advice, what is the point in paying me?' Culligan asked boldly.

'I begin to wonder that myself, sir,' I answered sharply.

'What I mean to say is,' he said quickly, seeing his sole client drifting from him, 'that would absolutely secure custody, but if you don't care for the fellow. . . . May I enquire what is amiss with him, that you are turning down a fortune?'

'No, you may not, Mr Culligan.'

'He has red and green marble fireplaces, you see,' Mama told him, as I had made a few jokes at home about these monstrosities.

'I see,' Culligan said, weighing this information carefully. 'Red and green, eh? Sounds a queer nabs, but I cannot think red and green fireplaces would disqualify him as a good father.

Happen he is color blind – no stain on a man's character.'

'You can forget Mr Everett and marriage,' I said firmly.

'There goes our normal family unit, then,' he answered, throwing up his hands. 'Unless *you* have a parti in your eye?' he asked my mother.

'Really, Mr Culligan! I am a *widow*,' she said, incensed.

'If Menrod's man twigs to these precedents, you may be sure his lordship will get himself shackled up quick as winking, and your chances are nil.'

'If he wants them that badly, he may have them,' I said, arising.

'Let us not be hasty,' Culligan said in a placating manner, tilting his ginger head to one side and pointing me back to my chair, with one not overly clean finger. 'There's ways and ways of handling the situation. I'm all for dealing aboveboard when I can, but there's no denying not every engagement ends at the altar. If you were seen by the court to be on the verge of a marriage, it might serve as well as the sacrament itself.'

'Mr Culligan – you cannot be serious! I would not do such a scaly thing to Mr Everett. That is an impossibly low stunt, to let on you are going to marry a man, then back out after he has served his purpose. Really, it is enough to make me question your ethics.'

'I did not mean to imply you keep the gentleman in the dark as to your true intentions, Miss Harris. If he's close enough he's offered marriage, then it stands to reason he might be fond enough of you to go along with the trick. There would be some as would look askance at the advice I am giving you, but it is not my job to give you moral lessons, only practical advice as to how you might legally accomplish what you set out to, do you see?'

'Yes, I see very well, and I don't like it.'

'Liking it is not the point. Between you and me and the

hatter's block, *I* don't like what you are about, but that is neither here nor there. You are my client, and every client deserves to have his case heard in a court of law, even the worst sort of criminals.'

'I hope I am not a criminal!'

'Where would them kiddies be better off, in a castle where they would be treated like lords and ladies, or in a tumbledown cottage, with no prospects before them? *You* tell *me*, Miss Harris,' he demanded severely.

'In a tumbledown cottage,' I answered instantly.

'Well, then, think it over, what I suggested. Don't say no till you have talked it over with your gentleman friend. He might look on it as a very good joke on Menrod. He would feel it helpful in winning your hand too. You could lead him on. . . .'

'Please – say no more about it. This is out of the question.'

'I think he *would* do it, Gwendolyn. He is very obliging,' Mama reminded me.

'What is out of the question today is often acceptable the next day. Meanwhile, I'll continue with my work here, and inform you if I can get a witness to testify against Menrod's character.'

'I have asked you *not* to broadcast any tasteless questions about Lord Menrod.'

'I have assured you of my subtlety, ma'am. I know what I am about. I'll not run afoul of the law again – er . . . and by the way,' he ran on, blushing at his slip, 'there was a trip to London necessary in the course of my investigations. I have itemized it here. . . .' He shoved a long sheet at me.

'Chancery is in London,' he mentioned.

This sounded reasonable, more reasonable than putting up at the Clarendon Hotel, one of the most expensive in the city. I took him to task about it, and sliced his bill in half. 'I am not a flat, Mr Culligan. I know what a night in London costs. Don't think to line your pockets at my expense. I would suggest you repair your cuffs, however. It will do me no good to be represented in court by a man in tatters. Good day.

'I believe we ought to change lawyers, Mama. What do you think? I don't like the cut of him above half,' I said as soon as we had left.

'It would be so very dear, having to send another man off to London, when Culligan has already been there. He does have a sly way about him,' she added, but in no condemnatory way.

'He is a crook, suggesting I use Mr Everett so poorly.'

'You would have to marry him if you told them in court you meant to. It would certainly solve all our problems,' she added, with a weary sigh.

'It wouldn't solve them; it would only change them.'

Our visit to Culligan was followed by a couple of fairly dull days. Mr Everett came to call once. I did not mention Culligan's idea of rigging up a spurious engagement to him, and by a judicious lowering of my brows every time she tried to broach the matter, I also restrained my mother from doing so. We did not go up to the Manor to see the children, nor were they sent down to visit us. Menrod had other things on his mind. He was busy getting his local mistress packed off. We learned from Mr Everett that Mrs Livingstone had left the neighborhood very suddenly.

'I cannot imagine what accounts for it,' he said, inserting a gold toothpick he carries in his pocket into his mouth, but only to gnaw on it. He is not so vulgar as to put it to its rightful use in a polite sitting room. 'You would think when he has had all the expense of keeping her here year round, he would not send her away when he finally comes to make a visit, and would have some use from her.'

'It is clear why he did it. He is trying to whitewash his character, to hide from Chancery that he is a rake,' I explained.

'Mr Culligan thinks. . . .' Mama said, with a determined set to her features.

'Would you care for a cup of tea, Mr Everett?' I intervened swiftly.

'That would be dandy.'

Shortly after we had taken tea, he left, and shortly after he left, Menrod arrived, alone.

'Good afternoon. Why did you not bring the children with you?' I asked.

'What I have to say is not for young ears. Yours will be burning before I am done,' he cautioned. Mama gave a few longing looks at the door, but kept to her chair.

'Please do not feel it necessary to speak to us about having turned off your mistress,' I answered loftily. 'It was well done of you to remove your Magdalene from the parish. Futile to your purpose, but well done. Her three-year residence will be sufficient to establish your character, without actually having her on hand.'

'These efforts you have undertaken to establish my base character had better stop, or you will be extremely sorry.'

'You heard that threat, Mama, in case any corroboration should be necessary in court?' I mentioned to my mother.

'I must speak to Pudge,' was the support I received from her. She got out of her chair so fast she nearly tripped on her skirts. It was not necessary for Menrod to arise, as he had not yet taken a seat. He found it more intimidating to stand glowering above me, throwing his arms about wildly.

'It is not an empty threat,' he announced, his dark eyes afire with anger. 'If that weasel of a Culligan comes snooping around my home again, asking impertinent questions of my servants, he will receive the thrashing he deserves. You are his employer. I hold *you* responsible for this outrage.'

'Do have a seat, Menrod. You can rant as well sitting down.'

He cast an angry glance on me, then sat down. 'Now perhaps you will tell me what you are talking about.'

'I am talking about your employee questioning my servant girls regarding my behavior to them – whether I have *ever* *forced* them to have relations with me, whether I *beat* them, pay them their salaries, and other such questions as are an insult to a man of honor. If he were worth killing, I would call him out. I would not lower myself to take him so seriously.'

'I see.' My suspicions were confirmed; despite my strict orders not to pursue this unsavory course, Culligan had done it. 'Is it outraged innocence or is it guilt that has you in this almighty pelter? It is a strong reaction, surely, to speak of a challenge.'

'I will not have my integrity impugned in this unspeakable manner. You will call off your mutt or be liable for the consequences. It is entirely up to you, but I tell you in all earnestness, Miss Harris, if another incident of this sort occurs, you will be sued for slander.'

'From what you tell me, you were not accused of anything. Can it possibly be illegal to ask a question?'

'Such questions as were posed to my people were an assault on my good name. The very fact of their being raised gives rise to doubts. They are simple, innocent folks, and when the questions are also the subject of gossip in town, where Culligan has been prying, it lends a hint of substance to them.'

'I daresay Mrs Livingstone too could be called more than a *hint* of substance,' I pointed out dutifully.

'What arrangements I make for my private, personal life are no concern of yours or anyone else's.'

'Why did you find it necessary to turn her off, then?'

'Mrs Livingstone has gone to visit friends at Brighton. She will be returning shortly.'

'Not before six weeks, I wager.'

'Two can play at this game,' was his next statement. 'How would you like it if I began asking around town whether it is true you and Everett slip away to London for a weekend every month? Would you find that amusing, as your smirks tell me you enjoy my dilemma? Of course there is no truth in it, so far as I know, but once the question is abroad, you know, folks begin remembering there is no smoke without fire. They will recall having seen his carriage pass through town, headed toward the city, with more than one person in it. Someone else will remember the bonnet looked very like Miss Harris's, and before twenty-four hours are up, you have become a scarlet woman.'

'It is impossible to prove an innocent person guilty. My weekends are all accounted for. I am always in town on Saturdays, and in church on Sundays.'

'Are you telling me you don't mean to call him off?'

'I didn't sic Culligan on you. I told him *not* to follow that tack, when he suggested it. I'll speak to him.'

'You might have known when you hired a man of that kidney what would result.'

'It happens Sir Nathan did not offer me his valuable services gratis. I do not approve of these questions Culligan has been asking, but for the rest, your personal conduct is a valid point to be raised in the case. You think so too, or you would not have gotten rid of Mrs Livingstone.'

'A precaution merely. I will leave no stone unturned to secure guardianship of my niece and nephew. Every trip I make to this cottage confirms me in my belief they would be poorly off here. Your lack of judgment, quite as much as your oft-lamented lack of funds, would be to their detriment. I wish you will reconsider your decision.'

'Every trip you make here confirms in my mind that I too was correct. You are *bribing* them to like you, with wooden horses and bags of sugarplums. You consider yourself above the law. Because you have taken into your head they would be a congenial amusement for a few weeks, you think by some divine right of peers you ought to have them, automatically. That I, with perfectly equal claims so far as kinship goes, *even question* your whim has got you outraged. I *have* reconsidered my decision, Menrod. I am more convinced than ever that you would make a perfectly wretched guardian. I used to think it a pity your interest would be so short-lived; I come to see the only hope for their living a normal life is your losing all interest as soon as possible, and turning them over to servants. But then, without the comfort of a Mrs Livingstone nearby, no doubt you will soon be darting back to London. Good day.'

'You will be happy to hear I am to spend the entire spring at the Manor. Good day to you, Miss Harris.'

He arose and strutted from the room at a gait similar to Mr Everett's with his knees very stiff. His eyes glanced with satisfaction to the left, where the stairs were returned to their former gloominess.

I dashed a terse note off to Culligan, informing him that if he continued with the course I had forbidden, he could consider himself dismissed.

# Chapter Nine

$\mathcal{T}$ he next morning, we received a call from the Dowager Lady Menrod. She brought the children with her, which was no more than a pretext. Her real motive was to hint there was a match brewing between her cousin and her stepson.

'Menrod has taken the decision to spend a few months at home,' she announced happily. 'Lady Althea was to return to London, but has sent off instead for some lighter clothing and her mount. She will be riding with Menrod. They are both fond of riding. I am to have a little ball next month, at the Manor. Menrod tells us the Dower House is too small.'

The children were not greatly interested in these bits of gossip. Ralph had squeezed himself in beside me on a chair built for one, while Gwen sat waiting for some attention.

'Lady Althea is making me a new gown for my doll,' she announced, glancing around the room for some reaction to this stunning intelligence.

'Such a beautiful doll her uncle bought her in London, with real hair,' Lady Menrod said, smiling on the child.

'But I take Goldie to bed with me,' Gwen confided. 'She is softer, and it doesn't matter if her gown gets mussed.'

I only half listened to her. It occurred to me that the reason for Mrs Livingstone's holiday was not as I first thought. It was the quest for Lady Althea's hand that accounted for it. It was not long dawning on me that the new match had another reason than the birth of love between the two principals. Lady Althea had been coming to the neighborhood forever with no luck. If Menrod was proving amenable to her charms now, it was because he had discovered those precedents spoken of by Culligan, and was getting himself a wife to establish the necessary family unit.

A panic surged in my breast. He had all the other advantages – in birth, social position, wealth, he out-classed me. If he meant to offer a wife as well, my slight chances for success dwindled toward zero.

'Will you read me a story?' Ralph asked.

'There is company present, Ralph. I cannot do it now.'

'We could go upstairs in the big chair,' he pointed out.

When he repeated his request a moment later, Lady Menrod was obliging enough to excuse us. 'Read to him if you wish, Miss Harris. He is always pestering Lady Althea to read him stories.'

This frightening statement got us up the stairs very quickly. He snuggled cosily on to my lap.

'Do you often see Lady Althea?' I asked.

'Sometimes. Nobody reads to me at home. There are books there, to look at the pictures.'

I had a vision of the poor tyke, sitting alone, thumbing disconsolately through books while I sat alone at the cottage here, missing him. It was dreadfully unfair, and that Lady Althea was usurping my rightful place was even worse.

I could read only a short story on that day, because of the company below. 'What will you do when you go home?' I asked, feeling a wave of pity and grief to see him go.

'Uncle is going to look for a pony for me.'

'A live pony! Oh, Ralph, you are too young.'

'Uncle says he and Papa rode young, so I am to have a

mount. I will call him Rufus. That was Papa's mount's name in India.'

'Aren't you afraid?'

'No, I am not afraid,' he answered gallantly, but afraid or not, I thought it a dangerous venture, to put a child on a mount. 'I asked Uncle if I could have a live pony, since I can ride the wooden one now.'

This smacked of bribery, buying them anything they wanted, without thought to the possible consequences.

Tea had been served during our absence. The guests were preparing to leave. 'Come along, Ralph,' Lady Menrod called. 'Cousin Althea is going to take you children into the village this afternoon, after she and Menrod are back from their drive.'

'She is going to buy us some ices,' Gwen said contentedly. More bribery!

'We will have a cake next time you come,' I told her, to get in on the bribery myself.

'I like it with whipped cream.'

After they had left, I sat down with my mother to discuss the visit. 'You know what this is all about. Menrod will offer for Lady Althea in order to have a mother to put forward in Chancery.'

'How sly of him! Now you *must* have Mr Everett, Gwendolyn.'

'Don't tempt me.'

'It would be an excellent match, getting us out of this dark, draughty cottage. But such magnificence at Oakdene; I am not sure I could ever become accustomed to it.'

'You could buy yourself a pair of green glasses, to cut down on the glare.'

'Ah, well, I don't suppose Menrod has any real notion of offering for Lady Althea. It is all a ruse, of the sort Culligan tried to push on you, letting on to marry, for the looks of it.'

'If that is his trick, you may be sure Althea knows nothing of it. She means business. Lady Menrod certainly thinks it will come to a match. He is of worse character than I thought, if that is what he is up to. I wonder if it is.'

'What bothers me is the ball. I daresay it is to publicize the match. You don't suppose they will take into their heads to invite *us*?'

'I should hope so indeed! How could they possibly not, when we are connected to Menrod? There is no reason to miss out on an excellent party only because of the legal battle. I shall certainly attend if we are asked.'

'I could always say I have a migraine.'

'Mama, don't be such a peagoose. You will not be expected to stand up with him. You can sit and play cards with your friends.'

'I can do that at home, without having to buy a new gown and be perfectly miserable at the Manor.'

'Why should you be miserable?'

'It is so very fine, with all those carpets one is afraid to step on, and the upholstery so historical it would be a crime if you spilled a drop of wine, and one is bound to do it, when she knows she must not.'

'You didn't feel this hesitation to dine at Oakdene. The Manor could not possibly be more richly appointed than that.'

'It is not the same. You can feel so very comfortable with Mr Everett. Menrod is always *angry* about everything; Mr Everett is never angry. I never met a better-natured man, excepting your papa, who was a saint. It is no small thing to find a good natured husband, Gwendolyn. The best-looking fellows grow fat and bald in the end, like the homely ones, and what you are left with is their natures. When you marry, be sure you find a good-natured man. Like Mr Everett,' she added slyly.

I actually considered this course for a few moments. One would always be very comfortable with him, as she mentioned, except when it was necessary to be seen with him in high company. For him to be telling guests how much he paid for everything would be an embarrassment. One would be surrounded with every luxury imaginable. A bright, secure, rich future danced before my eyes. Then Mr Everett danced stiff-kneed into the picture, making it all impossible. The only possible marriage I could envisage with him was a marriage of convenience, one that allowed me complete absence from his bed. I doubted even his good nature extended that far, however.

'Well, what do you say?' she asked hopefully.

'I don't know why I cannot bring myself to accept him. I need a good shaking, don't I? It is just that he is so common in his ways – unrefined.'

'We could polish up his manners, between the two of us.'

'Yes, he is very biddable. He removed two of his fobs from his watch chain as soon as ever I mentioned them. I daresay he could be transformed into a fine gentleman, with some coaxing.'

Mrs Pudge had strolled in during my speech, and had to hear what was being discussed. 'What you are faced with is what Christian encountered on his pilgrim. You have your neighbor Obstinate, being Menrod, and your neighbor Pliable, being Everett.'

'Which did Christian choose?' Mama asked.

'He had the good sense to spurn both of them. Nobody wants too pliable a man, for he don't stand for anything. He can be talked hither and thither at a whim. An obstinate man, on the other hand, won't listen to good reason. There's little enough to choose betwixt and between them. You're better off an old maid, miss.'

'There was no question of my receiving an offer from Neighbor Obstinate, Mrs Pudge. That was not the point.'

'That's something, anyways,' she said, and left to nag her

pliable spouse into washing the dining-room windows.

I gave no thought to her sanctimonious mutterings. She had become like a squeaky door, always whining but little heeded. That evening, after dinner, Mr Everett dropped in for a visit. His first talk was of architecture, some new moldings that were being installed in the kitchen. Before long, he broached a more interesting subject.

'What do you think of the scandal about Menrod?' he asked calmly.

'What scandal?' I demanded at once, every sense alive with curiosity.

'Why, the kitchen girl at the Manor he has got in the family way. Shocking thing, a man in his position. He ought to be horsewhipped. He shuffled her off home to her family at Newbury, but it was his work. That will serve your case well, Gwendolyn.' He had slipped into using my first name at Oakdene, and continued it regularly without censure now.

'He has only been home a little over a week. It cannot have happened so soon.'

'It happened five months ago, from what they are saying in town. She was sent home two months ago, before her condition became obvious. To turn her from the door is worse than the rest. He ought to have shown more responsibility,' he condemned.

'I cannot believe it of Menrod,' I said. He kept a mistress, but to treat his helpless servants so was worse. He did not have a reputation of that sort.

'He was not home five months ago, was he, Mama?' I asked.

'When would that be – around the end of October?' she asked, doing the required calculations.

'About that time, yes. He was home last summer for two weeks. He dropped in for a day or two at Christmas as well.'

'Summer was too early, and Christmas too late. They have

got the date of it wrong,' she decided.

'They have got the paternity wrong. Which girl was it?' I asked Everett.

'A squinty redhead is what I heard,' Everett answered. 'Nel something or other was her name. Nel Scott, I think.'

'That ugly patch who was hired a year ago? He would not touch her with a pair of tongs. This must be a joke,' I declared, incredulous.

'All cats are gray in the dark, as they say,' Everett mentioned.

'No joke for her, poor girl,' Mama said.

'It is Culligan's questions that have put this idea into circulation. This is really too bad of him.' A worry equally as great as the inequity of traducing Menrod was what he would say, or do, when he heard about it. If he wanted those children badly enough to marry Lady Althea, he must want them very badly indeed. I knew, as I sat talking to Everett, *I* would not marry to inherit the whole country, let alone two children, only one of whom I truly loved.

'Very likely it is,' Everett agreed. 'You don't believe it of him, then, Gwendolyn?'

'No, I do not. I will change solicitors. I shall disassociate myself from that muckraker entirely.'

'I formed a poor opinion of the man myself,' he admitted.

The damage was done, but my displeasure might indicate to the neighborhood my opinion of the man who started the rumor. I sat in some trepidation of Menrod's next visit, and none at all of Everett's unnoticed remark that he had formed a poor opinion of Mr Culligan. When Menrod came to the cottage the next day, I learned my error. It was not the Nel Scott scandal that brought him, but something else; namely, my 'engagement' to Mr Everett.

# Chapter Ten

Lord Menrod came stomping to the cottage door fairly early in the morning. I was at work in my conservatory. The ministration of my plant family is generally my first occupation of the day. I go there immediately from breakfast to tend them before beginning less pleasant duties. I was in hands with some messy repotting work when he arrived. My aspidistra was ready for a larger home than the eight-inch crockery pot in which it resided at the time.

Mrs Pudge brought him to me. 'Your mother is up in the cheese room, rotating the cheeses, so his lordship says he'll talk to you,' was her countrified manner of announcing our guest.

There was no trusting the smile Menrod wore. Had it been satirical, I would have expected a hot blast of vituperation to follow soon. It was nothing of the sort. He looked genuinely amused, so unusual an expression to be seen on his dour face that I demanded an explanation for it.

'Why, one does not come to offer congratulations, wearing a frown, Miss Harris,' he replied. He looked around at my specimens, selected a rattan chair, and waited for me to be seated. I remained standing. 'You spend a good deal of time here, I think?' he asked patiently. 'You might be a personification of Spring, amidst all this verdure. Quite the symbol of a spring day.'

'I more usually think of you as a whole month of spring – March, with its gusty howls. I mistrust your coming in like a lamb this morning. It hints at a more ferocious departure.'

'I fully expect we will be drawing our daggers before I leave, but we will do it elsewhere, so as not to shock your plants.'

'Kind of you. They are not accustomed to much violence, which is why I prefer them to most people. They are never ill-natured or abusive. They behave themselves with great propriety, and prosper with a little tending and affection.'

'*Affection?*' he asked, his eyes widening. 'Who would not?'

'Care, is what I mean.'

'When a lady begins to lavish her scanty affections on a *plant*, it augurs some unhinging of the mental faculties. I begin to comprehend the announcement in this morning's paper.'

'What announcement is that?' I asked, noticing he carried the Reading journal.

He handed it to me, folded with page three at the front. He pointed to a small article in the gossipy part of the sheet, which is called the 'Social Notes.' I read with considerable astonishment that Mrs Harris was happy to announce the betrothal of her daughter Gwendolyn to Mr Everett, of Oakdene, Reading. No words were possible. I just stared, my mouth opening and closing like a newly-hatched sparrow.

'Your shame is not of the sort forecast by me after all,' he rattled on easily, enjoying himself very much. 'No suspicious weekends in London after all, eh, Miss Harris? Tell me, am I to congratulate or commiserate with you on the announcement? It appears to have taken you by surprise.'

'This is impossible! There is some mistake! I have not accepted Mr Everett's offer. Who did this? Menrod – is this *your* work?' I asked, with some temporary derangement of the brain.

'No, no. A few weekends with him in London was the best I had to offer. Word of it must have gotten around, and he is doing the right thing by you.' His thin lips were stretched wide in a smile. His eyes were crinkled at the edges with laughter.

'He would never have undertaken to have published this without my consent. I *told* him I did not accept, very positively.'

'He actually did offer, did he? I half thought it was only a threat, to make me hand over my children.'

'They are not *your* children. They are *ours*.'

'A novel notion – but it is Everett who has won your hand.'

'Mine as much as yours, is what I meant,' I added hastily, as his smile stretched ever broader at my incoherence.

'What a delightful mystery. Who can have done it?' he asked, his curiosity piqued.

'It must be Mama. I'll go up to her this instant.'

I dashed out of the conservatory, up the demmed dark, low stairway to the cheese room, under the eaves. I did not notice Menrod had taken upon himself to follow, till I heard his head bump on the tamarack beam, and heard the undignified expletive that followed the accident.

'You must excuse our stairway. It was used to be brighter, till our landlord took the ludicrous idea to enclose it.'

'People must have been shorter two hundred years ago,' he mumbled.

The attic stairs have a greater clearance than the others. We got to the cheese room without further mishap. 'Mama, have you seen this?' I asked, shoving the newspaper into her hands.

She took it, read, frowned, then smiled beatifically. 'So you have come to your senses at last and accepted him. Good. I could not be happier. That will teach Men—' Menrod reached the top of the stairs at that point. I was six stairs before him. She came to an embarrassed halt. 'I thought you were alone, Gwendolyn,' she said.

'Menrod brought the paper to me. You did not send this notice in to them?'

'I? How should I? I didn't know a thing about it till you showed me this. But there is no harm in an announcement after all. We would have had to do it sooner or later.'

'I am not engaged! I told you I don't plan to marry him. Who could have done it?'

'Mr Culligan?' Menrod suggested mischievously.

'That's who it was. I shall drive straight into Reading and fire him.'

I turned sharply and bounded down the stairs, along the hall to the next set of stairs. I heard Menrod coming after me, hastening his steps, but did not wait for him. His bump on the flight down was harder than on the way up, because of our haste. I really feared, or hoped, he had knocked himself out. He was sent reeling back, and wore a red mark on his forehead when he reached the landing.

'You forgot to duck. What a pity,' I exclaimed. He glared mutely while drawing out a handkerchief to dry his forehead for blood. Finding none, he said, 'It is nothing. A tap only. You are going to Reading now, at once?'

'The sooner the better.'

'I am headed that way myself. I shall take you.'

'Thank you. Your team will make better time than ours. I want my anger to be at full boil when I arrive.'

'My being in the carriage with you will assure it. Are you not going to wear a bonnet?' he asked, when I took a step toward the door without one.

'Of course I am.'

I went to the closet to fetch the necessary items, rammed my navy-blue felt on my head, accepted Menrod's help with my pelisse, and went out the door.

'I shall sue him. Is it possible to sue a lawyer?' I asked.

'Certainly it is. They are not above the law. It is also possible to knock their teeth down their throats.'

'I do not plan to attack him physically,' I said, as he held the carriage door for me.

'*I* owe him a little something as well. He has been propagating more than one unfounded rumor.'

'Oh, you mean about Nel Scott, I daresay. I hope you believe I had nothing to do with that odious lie. In fact, I ought to apologize, I suppose, though I had no way of knowing what he was about.'

'Yes, you ought.'

'I am sorry. I mean that, even if I am cross. It was an awful thing for him to do.'

'I accept your apology, even if I too am cross.'

After a few moments' cross silence, I asked, 'Who was the father, or do you know?'

'We have the culprit. A peddler she met in town. He would have married her, but for the problem of a wife and a few children at home. Another inaccuracy in the story is my having discharged her. She wanted to return to her family. It seems there was a lad so undemanding as to offer her marriage, despite her condition.'

'And her looks – the squint, I mean.'

'I did not see the groom, but if rumor is correct, he cannot afford to be choosy in the looks department. "A face like a bulldog," my footman told me. This is quite a place for peculiar matches, is it not?'

'Your own promises to be the only respectable alliance in town.'

'*My* marriage?' he asked, his supple brows lifting in two arches. 'I had best have another look at the newspaper. I stopped reading when I came to your notice.'

'I have not seen it announced publicly. When Lady Menrod spoke of the ball, and Lady Althea extending her visit, sending off for her mount, I thought. . . .'

'What?' he demanded, staring wildly.

'Lady Menrod said . . . actually, she did not say anything about a wedding. We only assumed that as her cousin is to extend her visit at the same time as you are at home, there must be a wedding in prospect.'

'It is the first thing I have heard about it.'

'It was just a surmise.'

'I mean about extending the visit, and having a ball. They will want to use the Manor for that.'

I did not tell him of his stepmother's duplicity, her telling us he had offered the use of the Manor. 'Of course the length of her visit is nothing to me,' he went on. 'She is my stepmother's guest, not mine.'

I examined him closely, wondering if I had misjudged the man. If he was telling the truth, and his enthusiastic tone suggested he was, then he was not planning to form a family unit to get the children after all. I would not mention Culligan's precedents to him, in case he was unaware of the efficacy of this ploy.

While I had his ear, I determined to discover whether he, unlike I, had any letters from Peter indicating the father's wish that Menrod stand guardian, in case of an early death. Later on, I said, very casually, 'Did you hear often from Peter when he was in India?'

'No, he was an indifferent correspondent. He dropped a note from time to time. You heard often from your sister, I should think?' There was a wariness about him that warned me he was angling for the same information as myself.

'Yes, great, lengthy epistles, telling us everything.'

'Did you keep them?'

'Yes, I read them often still. They are full of interesting stories about India.'

His wariness increased. 'I would be interested to read them, if you have no objections?' he suggested tentatively.

I swallowed my smile as best I could. 'Save yourself the bother. There is no mention of the children coming to Mama and me, in case she should die. That is what you wish to discover, I know.'

'I don't suppose you were truly interested to know what kind of a correspondent Peter was either.'

'Not in the least. Am I correct to conclude you have nothing in writing indicating his wishes in the matter?'

'Nothing. He was so young, he had not thought of death at all. It was a great tragedy, was it not, the two of them going down together in that boat? It was supposed to be a pleasure cruise. You never know when your turn is coming up, hiding around the bend, to snatch you.'

An uncontrolable shudder seized me at his lugubrious talk. 'Must you be so morose? Here it is a beautiful spring day, and all you can speak of is dying.'

'We can speak of anything you like. I just happened to make one comment about death. It is not something you can hide from, you know. It is coming to us all.'

'Not for a few years yet, I hope.'

'You know not the day nor the hour.'

'You are beginning to sound like Mrs Pudge.'

'I had not taken her for such a wise woman. I believe it is why men and women marry and have children, in a futile effort to cheat death, to have some bit of themselves still alive in the world. It is very likely why you are so fond of your namesake, Gwendolyn, and why I have become so quickly attached to Ralph. He looks much as I did when I was a child, you know. The dark Hazelton coloring, with something of his mother in his withdrawn nature.'

'Ralph is not withdrawn,' I answered quickly, but did not correct him as to my great love for my namesake. 'He is very personable, easy to talk to, once you get to know him. Hettie used to write that he was rambunctious. It is his parents' deaths that has made him a little shy.'

'He is more girlish than is good for a boy. It could become a serious problem for him later, when he has to go to school. He takes well to sports, though.'

'To riding in particular?'

'Yes, that was my meaning.'

'He is much too young to be put on horseback.'

'Pony back is all he will be put on for a few years yet.'

'I still think he is too young, but I don't expect you to listen to anything I have to say.'

'I don't pretend to be an expert on children. I would be interested to hear your opinions, particularly with regard to Gwen.'

The only thing I had to say about her was that she was a saucy baggage, and I could hardly say that. 'She is a great favorite with her grandma, because of her resemblance to Hettie. She has a winning manner.'

'She has, and is well aware of it, despite her youth. She has already cozened me into providing her with an unending supply of sweets, though I know perfectly well they are not good for her. I don't mean to spoil the child, however, if that is what you are thinking.'

'No irreparable harm will be done in six weeks.'

This remark caused some constraint to settle over us. I used the silence to form my plans. I preferred that Menrod not accompany me to Culligan's office. The reason for the engagement notice would arise, and it was not something I wished my opponent to be aware of. A visit to Oakdene was also essential. I would ask him to let me off at Culligan's office, and hire a hackney cab to take me to Oakdene, from which spot Mr Everett would see me home.

'You can drop me off here,' I said as we entered the block of Reading where my solicitor had his shabby office.

'Drop you off? My business is with Culligan too.'

'Oh.'

We alit together, walking slowly to the doorway, while Menrod surveyed the squalid surroundings, his lip curled in distaste. 'Whatever made you select this fellow?' he asked.

'He came highly recommended,' I replied, quickening my steps past the mangy cat with a cod's head between his teeth, the dusty windows, from which a toothless hag peered out, the knobless door.

'You could break your neck here,' he went on complaining as we felt our way up the dark, steep steps to the second story.

'I have learned to handle a dark stairway.'

Culligan removed his boots from his desk top when we entered, to make us welcome. He neither recognized Menrod nor gave me time to introduce him. 'You have come to congratulate me,' was his smiling speech. 'All a part of the job. We'll get those kiddies away from their uncle yet, see if we don't, Miss Harris. You've heard what is being said of him? All the rumors set afoot without the need of an outright lie being told.'

'This is Lord Menrod,' I said quickly, before he should start on any other outrage.

'Eh?' he asked, his green eyes opening an inch wider.

'Lord Menrod, I would like you to meet my solicitor,' I said, emphasizing the name, to be sure Culligan understood.

'An honor and a pleasure to make your acquaintance, sir,' Culligan said promptly, sticking his hand across the desk, with his cuffs still in tatters. Menrod stared at the hand but made no move to touch it.

'You will be receiving a letter from Sir Nathan Beckwith very soon,' Menrod told him, his voice so cold, the icicles formed in the air. 'In the meanwhile, if there are any more of these unfounded rumors about me put in circulation, you had better put them to rest, or I will be obliged to mutilate you. We came to tell you your services are no longer required. Good day.'

He then put a hand on my elbow and pulled me toward the door, while I had a dozen more things I wanted to say to Culligan, most particularly to discover about the announcement in the paper.

'You've not paid me for my latest work!' Culligan howled, with an accusing look at me.

'Did you bring your pistol with you, Miss Harris?' Menrod asked.

'I have to find out about the engagement,' I said aside to Menrod. He stopped his dash to the door but looked extremely impatient.

'Was it you who put that article about Mr Everett and me in today's paper?' I asked bluntly.

His face squeezed up in concentration, as he rapidly figured the pros and cons of the act. 'I might have been instrumental,' he hedged cautiously.

'A simple yes or no is all that is required.'

'Mr Everett actually had it done,' he admitted, while scrutinizing my face for a reaction.

'Lucky for you,' Menrod growled, then continued to the exit, dragging me most uncomfortably by the elbow.

'I'll send you a bill,' Culligan called after us.

'Save yourself the paper. There will be no payment,' Menrod called back, without slackening his steps.

'Everett has a lot of gall. Oakdene will be our next step, I assume?' he asked, as we felt our way down the steps.

'There is no need for you to come.'

'It's a long walk. You came in my carriage.'

'I can hire a hackney.'

We had reached the bottom of the stairs. He pushed the door open. The cat, now without the cod's head, slithered in past us.

'Another client for Culligan,' Menrod remarked. 'I was going to bash his teeth in, but dislike to give fuel to the rumors he is spreading. The best course is to ignore them.'

'I wonder if he was telling the truth about Mr Everett sending that notice in.'

'He wouldn't tell the truth about his name, unless he saw some advantage in it. I still cannot conceive what took you to him. Once glance at his setup must have told you what he is.'

'Let me solve the great mystery for you, once for all. What he is, Menrod, is *cheap*, or so I believed when I went to him. He was the best we could afford.'

'It might turn out to be the most expensive bargain you *ever* made.'

'What do you mean? Are you going to sue him? Surely I cannot be held accountable for his actions! I am only his client.'

'You had best get in writing today you are no longer his client.'

'You *are* going to sue, then?'

'I always follow my solicitor's advice. I shall wait to hear what Sir Nathan has to say. If there is any question of your responsibility, of course I shan't prosecute.'

'That is generous of you,' I said, impressed by his gallantry.

'Generous? You can't get blood from a stone. You have no money.'

'Neither has Culligan.'

'Well, then, if you insist, I am the soul of generosity. I am also gentleman enough to feel churlish at doing battle with a poor, in the monetary sense, defenseless, and nearly witless lady.' This brash speech was accompanied by an arch smile. 'Won't you consider dropping the case, and let us be friends?'

'No, but I will rescind my compliment on your generosity.'

'We'll talk this out later. We cannot have a good shouting argument in the middle of the street.'

# Chapter Eleven

We entered the carriage to go on to Oakdene. The coming interview could not possibly be other than unpleasant. There was no one I would have preferred to be absent from it more than Menrod. What vulgarity would Everett not cop out into? He was so artless, he would say exactly what he was thinking, and what he thought was that he did me a great favor. I had figured out that Culligan had gone to him with the tale that an alleged coming marriage would help me, and Everett, so helpful, had gone along with it. How could I let him say such things in front of Menrod, and how could I prevent him? I would announce frankly we desired to talk in private. There was plenty to entertain the other guest for a few minutes in the saloon while we talked elsewhere. Gracious, there was enough finery to entertain him for a fortnight.

'He's overplanted,' was Menrod's comment on the parkland as we entered the grounds of Oakdene. There was a superfluity of young trees, not appearing excessive at their present diminutive size, but as they matured, the parkland would resemble a jungle.

All of the house's excesses appeared greater than before, when I entered with my companion. Servants got up in red livery with gold lace did seem almost comical, out in the country. The house I have already drawn for you. The few additions of carved trim went unnoticed. Everett was his usual stiff-kneed but genial self. He was delighted to see me, bewildered that I had brought the enemy along on my call, but willing to accept it.

'Step along into my saloon, and we'll have a glass of something wet,' he offered. 'What is your pleasure? I have got claret or sherry, orgeat, ratafia, brandy, champagne – you name it. Or a plain glass of home-brewed, if that is your pleasure, Lord Menrod. Maybe you'd prefer tea or coffee?'

I boggled under the surfeit of choices. 'Sherry will be fine,' Menrod decided for us all.

We had then to select whether to sit before a red fireplace or green, in the sun or shade, with fire or without. I sauntered to one of the choicer locations away from the fireplaces, giving us a view from the corner window.

'You have done yourself proud here,' Menrod said, glancing around. Such a leading statement earned him a tour of the room. He was complimentary to his host, without falling into flattery. The pictures particularly attracted his attention. He expressed approval of Everett's taste, which pleased the host immeasurably.

'I picked them all out myself,' he announced, beaming with pride. 'Not like the sofas and whatnot, that they sent around from the catalogue.'

'That must have saved you a good deal of time.'

'It did, but every one of the pictures was chosen by myself from an auction at Sotheby's, at a cost of £6,824.'

'You have good taste in paintings. I particularly admire the early Dutch pieces.'

'Dutch, are they? I made sure the lad said Flemish, but I have nothing against a Dutchman, so long as he pays his bills on time.'

I was happy to see Menrod behave himself like a gentleman.

I feared he would be patronizing. All the while they talked, I was aware that sooner or later the real purpose of our visit must come to the fore. As soon as Menrod emptied his glass, I said to them, 'Why do you not take another look at the paintings while Mr Everett and I have our private talk?'

'It would be the article in the morning's paper you refer to?' Everett asked.

'Yes,' I said, looking to Menrod sternly, to hint him away.

'May I help myself to another glass of your excellent sherry, Mr Everett?' he asked, purposely avoiding my stare.

'Drink up. There's plenty more where that came from. Sure you would not rather have champagne?'

'Quite sure, thank you. You spoil your guests.'

'I do my best by them,' Everett agreed, tilting the crystal decanter and filling all our glasses to the brim.

'About the announcement,' he ran on, oblivious to my quelling glances, 'you need not take it at face value, Gwendolyn. Between you and me and the bedpost, we both know what it means. Culligan is a rascal, not an inch of straight grain in him, but he came up with a proper clever idea there. If using my name as a prospective husband will help you win the kiddies, where is the harm in it? You need not feel obliged to have me if you don't like. And if you decide you do like, that is more than I look for. Well, when it comes down to it, I doubt you actually plan to marry the lady staying with your step-mother, either, eh, Lord Menrod? Despite she is a great lady, there's no denying she is a trifle long in the tooth for a younger fellow like yourself.'

'No, I don't plan to marry her,' Menrod agreed pleasantly.

'I knew it. A man in your position would not want such a well-aged piece when there's fresher fowl on the market.'

Menrod raised his glass, perhaps to hide the unsteadiness of his lips. Unaware of the social niceties, Everett continued his chatter. 'So there you are. Folks can engage in a legal battle tooth and nail, without necessarily falling out on a personal basis. Why, one of my best friends is a lad I beat out on the contract to supply lumber for a row of mill houses up north. We agreed on the sly between us, Rusty and myself, we'd not go below a certain price, and when it came down to it, he went down a guinea a load, and I went down a guinea and thruppence. With the quantity involved, thruppence a load was enough to give me the contract. I knew he'd go down a guinea, Rusty MacIvor. Knew to a penny what price he would ask, but he estimated wrong on me. Where do you buy your lumber, then, Lord Menrod?'

'I supply my needs from my own forest, and have it dressed at the local mill.'

'If you ever require ought that you don't have growing at home, don't hesitate to call on me. I can get you a good price, though I'm not active in the business any longer. I have contacts, you see.'

'I'll remember that.'

'About the announcement, Mr Everett,' I said, dismayed that it must be done publicly, but determined to do it, 'What shall I tell the papers?'

He threw up his callused hands. 'Nothing. Nothing at all. Let her ride. It is no one's business but our own. You can use me for as long as you need me. Six weeks, I think, is the time of the interim thing your friend, here, has got set up?'

'That's it. Six weeks,' Menrod confirmed.

'Happen you will have made up your mind one way or the other before then,' Everett suggested, with a roguish nod of his head at me.

'My mind *is* made up! I told you I did not wish to get married. It is extremely kind of you to have – have done this, though I wish you had not. Culligan was in touch with you?'

'Certainly he was. I hope I have not offended you, Gwendolyn. He came over the other night and put it to me straight. "The lady wants to let on she has a husband at the beck, but hasn't the nerve to ask you herself, so I am doing it for her," he said. I was happy to do it, and no need to feel obliged to me. Any time. We wrote up the notice and took it down to the newspaper office next morning.'

'You won't get a more generous offer than that,' Menrod pointed out, with a smile hovering at the back of his lips.

'The thing to do is to put in a retraction today, before the news is spread,' I said.

'That would do your case no good,' Everett pointed out.

'He's right,' Menrod agreed at once. 'It would give your character a tinge of frivolity, inconstancy, to play the jilt.'

'I would announce it was an *error*, not a jilting.'

Mr Everett looked uneasy. 'I wish you will reconsider,' he said mildly. 'The fact of the matter is, I have been along boasting of the match to a dozen or more of my best friends. I will look nohow if you announce it is all an error. Better to let it ride for the present, and fizzle out to a lover's quarrel in a few weeks – well, six weeks is all we're talking about.'

'Why do you not discuss it with your mother?' Menrod suggested, reading the indecision on my face.

I was anxious enough to leave that I grasped at the idea, though there was no doubt what she would advise me.

We arose to leave. In the end, I *thanked* Mr Everett for the impertinence of advertising an engagement that did not exist. It seemed the right thing to do. We were both urged to return at any time, to visit or tour the house or grounds, or anything we wished. Even hunting and fishing were urged on Menrod, a virtual stranger. Everett's good will was overwhelming.

'Pity I went to the expense of restocking my coverts last year,' Menrod said as we returned to his carriage. 'I believe the old fellow is lonesome. All that room, and he rattles around alone, but for the servants or any chance caller.'

'Like yourself at the Manor,' I pointed out.

'That was before I inherited Peter's children. Now my house is better filled.'

We drove down through the overplanted parkland to the road. Menrod wore a perplexed expression. 'Is something bothering you?' I asked.

'Yes, what puzzles me is that he wants to marry *you*.'

'Thank you very much.'

'That is not necessarily an insult. His taste, outside of his Dutch paintings, runs to the gaudy, overly ornate. I could picture him marrying three or four well-endowed actresses, or, say, a brace of Reubens-type ladies. There isn't enough of you to please him, and what there is is not. . . .' He had the wisdom to stop then.

'It is possible he judges people differently than he judges *things*.'

'That's possible. He didn't order you from a catalogue, at least. Still, if you mean to have him, you had better start beefing up. You'll be carrying ten or twenty pounds of diamonds, and yards of satin and lace, once he has control of you.'

'Oh, no! If I married him, I would restrain his exuberance for decoration.'

'You have given the matter serious consideration, I see. It is obvious what might attract you to him. He is an excellent parti. If you honed the rough edges a little, he is basically a sound fellow, good-natured, generous to a fault. As crooked as a dog's hind leg, but he is such a naïve cynic, we shan't quibble about that.'

'He is not crooked enough to keep his chicanery to himself.'

'You may be sure he kept it to himself till he got the contract for the mill houses sewn up tight.'

That was not what I referred to. It was the engagement, but I was tired of the subject, so did not correct him. Menrod left me off at the door at home. I thanked him civilly but did not invite him.

'You'll want to talk this newspaper business over with your mother. I shall be scanning the morrow's social page with interest, to learn what decision you come to.'

'Say hello to the children for me.'

'Why don't you come up sometime and say hello to them yourself?' he countered. 'No reason for us to be at odds only because of the legal battle. That was one good piece of advice from your friend.'

'I'll go up one day, to see how badly you are spoiling them,' I threatened.

'Do. I will be happy to spoil you too,' he answered. He tipped his hat, and the carriage lumbered off.

'What happened in town?' Mrs Pudge asked, before I got my bonnet off.

'I dispensed with Culligan's services. I must find a new solicitor. I wonder who I should get. I should have asked Menrod.'

'Menrod?' Mrs Pudge asked, her eyes swelling. 'I would as lief send my soul among lions. What deceit has he wrought, to have you talking so foolish? Menrod indeed!'

'He is not so bad.'

'He's cozened you with his flattering tongue, in other words. Flattering tongues ought to be cut off. His brother, Peter, the same with your poor sister, who's gone to her watery grave because of him. That pair of lads went astray as soon as they were born. Partaking with adulterers and all the rest of the tricks of heathendom. What about the engagement?'

'I shall inform you, Mrs Pudge, as soon as I have got it sorted out in my head.'

'In the papers is where you have got to get it sorted out.

We've had a dozen callers stopping by to congratulate you, while laughing up their sleeves at us.'

'How nice. Where is Mama?'

'She's washing that old black devil cat of Menrod's. I threw a bucket of slops on him, and she, the ninny, is washing him, and getting herself scratched to pieces for her trouble. I'll tell you, that cat is half warlock. He knows to an instant when Lady is let out, and pops up like clockwork to try his charms on her.'

'In the kitchen?' I asked.

'No, I put her out in the yard. I'll not have her making a mess in my clean kitchen. Pudge just washed my floor.' She crossed her arms over her apron, tilted herself back from the waist at a pugnacious angle to confront me.

'Thank you,' I said, and left her in that uncomfortable attitude. That woman is due for firing. I have caught the bug, from turning off Culligan.

I discussed the matter with my mother, the announcement in the paper, I mean. She thought it best to let it ride for the present, but to our few close friends, we would explain the true state of affairs. Our good friends were not Everett's close friends, so this was possible. Eventually it would all be forgotten.

'You would not want to embarrass him,' she reminded me.

I did not want to, either. It was remarkably generous of him to offer his services, with nothing in return but my lukewarm thanks.

# Chapter Twelve

We had some difficulty finding a new lawyer to represent our case. There is no shortage of them in the city, and no excess of clients, but word of Culligan's shady dealings had circulated amongst the legal community, giving them all a strong aversion to our cause. I concluded from various comments dropped that the main reason for our rejection was a fear of Menrod's wrath. The man we finally persuaded to handle the matter was a Mr Doyle, a man of good moral reputation, without a clever bone in his body. He would file the necessary papers in Chancery, outline what we had to offer, appear in person at the necessary time, but made perfectly clear he was not interested in any underhanded dealings.

'Neither are we,' I answered hotly. 'That is precisely why we turned Culligan off. Menrod was correct to suggest we change our man, don't you agree, Mama?' I slipped in, to see if the name's magic might be used for us, rather than against.

'You are on speaking terms with his lordship?' Mr Doyle enquired with interest.

'Speaking terms?' I asked, laughing lightly. 'Good gracious, we are friends and neighbors, as well as connections. This custody business has not interfered with our personal relationship. We see him nearly every day.'

After this slightly misleading statement, Mr Doyle saw his

way clear to handle our case, for a fee no higher than Culligan's. I regretted we had not gone to him in the first place.

After the main features had been discussed, I asked, 'Do you feel it would help the cause at all if I were married to a good, upright citizen?' I wished to discover whether Culligan knew what he was about, or had led me utterly astray.

'Marriage to the right man would help.' He nodded. 'You speak, of course, of your fiancé, Mr Everett. I read it in the papers. May I congratulate you, Miss Harris? It would give you a better chance. The material advantages you could then offer would be vastly increased, would match his lordship's, even. Good schooling would be provided, and ultimately the children might expect to inherit some part of the estate. It would do you no harm to rush the marriage forward, if you had not planned to do it before the case comes up for hearing.'

'My plans do not include an early marriage, but I daresay the engagement might. . . .'

'Oh, no. An engagement is no more than a prospect. Actualities are what the court is interested in. It is possible that the marriage would never occur, owing to death or accident, or even a change of mind. I know you think the last-named unlikely, but until you are Mrs Everett in law, the advantages of the match are in doubt, and will not be taken into considera-tion.'

'I see.'

'Without the marriage, I must tell you, your chances against what Lord Menrod has to offer are negligible. Everyone deserves to be represented, however, and I will be happy to represent your interests.'

'Thank you.'

'Shall I go forward, on the understanding that you will be Mrs Everett within the next month or so?'

'No, that is not at all likely.'

'Why not?' he asked, with a flush at his boldness.

'Because I do not plan to marry soon,' I answered unhelp-fully.

I feared the case was lost, and felt the accompanying sense of defeat. My spirits were not at all high as we drove home. They rose considerably to see Gwen and Ralph out playing under the great mulberry tree that robs our front windows of light and obstructs our view of the road but is a favorite for all that, as it supplies us with the makings of a tasty cordial. They came pelting toward the carriage as we alit.

'Aunt Althea brought us down,' Gwen said.

'*Aunt* Althea?' I asked, startled and displeased at the misnomer.

'She lets us call her Aunt. She is embroidering flowers and birds on my new nightgown. She is a good stitcher.'

A stab of jealousy entered my heart, to realize I was losing the children; they were slipping from me, inch by inch, every day they lived at the Manor. Ralph came up more slowly, always a little shy when he had been away for a while. While Gwen turned to chatter to Mama, Ralph smiled and said hello.

I took his hand to walk toward the house, asking him how he liked his new pony. 'Good,' he answered happily. 'Uncle Menrod said you are going to come up and see me ride.'

'Yes, I shall come soon.'

'When?'

'One of these days.'

'Today – this afternoon?' he asked.

I pointed out that as he had come to me today, it would not be appropriate for me to visit him. 'Not till tomorrow, then,' he said resignedly.

I had no real intention of going at all, but determined on the spot I would, the very next day. If their real aunt was more often about, they would be less likely to call strangers by my title.

No one had told me Mr Everett was also at the cottage. Dismay struck like a blow when I saw his curled beaver, cane, and gloves in the hallway. My private moments with Ralph were snatched from me. I had to go in and talk to Everett, while Mama, Lady Althea, and Gwen formed another circle. It seemed odd, to find Lady Althea and Mr Everett conversing so happily when we first entered.

'So here is the young fellow you are at such pains to get under your roof,' Everett said, tousling Ralph's black head. 'You are a lucky boy, know it?'

Ralph backed up a step to escape his rough hands, hid behind my skirts, actually. 'How are you enjoying yourself at the Manor, eh?' he went on noisily. A few similar questions followed, all of them unanswered.

'Shy rascal. He is not a moonling, I hope?' Everett asked.

I managed to keep my teeth over my tongue, barely. The others began to join in our talk. Mrs Pudge grudgingly passed tea. We none of us took much pleasure from the visit, except perhaps Lady Althea, who distributed a deal of noble conde-scension on Mr Everett, who accepted it with calm satisfaction, as his due.

'Menrod tells me he has been to Oakdene,' she said, when she had sorted out Everett's identity. 'He has been full of praise for your paintings ever since.'

'I have a few that are worth looking at,' he admitted modestly. 'Half a dozen or so Dutch ones his lordship was kind enough to praise to the skies. There's plenty more he did not see. French and Italian and even some home-brewed English pieces. I have got a dandy Gainsborough room upstairs, six or eight of his pretty scenes with ladies disporting themselves beneath trees. By jingo, there is one of the women resembles yourself, milady. The Frenchies give their women a more pleasing countenance, I believe,' he rattled on, heedless of any slight. 'Your Fragonards and Watteaus are my own particular favorites. I've a number of them, a goodly number.'

Lady Althea stared, but I must grant she had the breeding not to smile at his exuberance. 'You were in lumber, I believe, before coming to the neighborhood?' she asked politely.

'I was in lumber and lumber is in me, in my blood and bones. My pa was woodcutter for old Lord Magnus. I fair grew up in forests, and when I was a tad older, in the mills, learning how to dress and cure her. There's tricks in it, like any trade.'

'I'm sure there are. My father, Lord Malgrove, has extensive forests.'

'I know the Malgrove forests very well, but you've mostly pine and spruce, you see, which is not good hard wood, not prime stuff. An oak, now, is a noble bit of lumber. Hard as nails, with a dandy grain to her when she's cut and finished.'

'They are slow to grow, I believe.'

'They're quality. Quality isn't got in a fortnight. Like old families, they take generations to achieve their fiber.'

'Our lumber at Malgrove may be inferior, but the family's antiquity I can vouch for,' she answered. There was an air almost flirtatious about the woman, which surprised me. I had not seen her in a room with a man before, which perhaps accounted for the change. She was more lively, more smiling, used her fine green eyes more strategically than before. This would be the manner she adopted in her pursuit of Menrod.

'It shows in the way you carry yourself,' he answered. 'Proud, like a queen.'

She flushed with pleasure. 'Thank you, sir. I am most curious about this Gainsborough lady who bears a resemblance to me. Several of my older relatives sat for him. It is possible you have got hold of some of my family's portraits. Do you know the title of the piece, off hand?'

'I couldn't tell you that. I know I paid two hundred and fifty for her. I'm not much of a one for names, to tell the truth, unless there is some special significance in it. I know I have the likeness of Miss Priscilla Dunker, for I sold her pa several yards of cherry to line his study, and saw the woman when she was young. She was a looker. Reynolds it is by, not Gainsborough.'

'You must find out the name and let me know.'

'We can go and check it out this minute if you'd care to,' he offered, on the spot. 'I could dash you there and back in two whisks of the cat's tail. You'd not even be late home for your luncheon.'

'Shall we?' she asked, smiling brightly. 'Would you care to come with us, Miss Harris? I don't want you to think I am stealing your beau.'

'Why do you not leave the children with me, and pick them up on your way home?' I suggested instead.

'*I* would like to see Oakdene,' Gwen stated loudly. 'Uncle Menrod said it is stuffed to the roof with treasures.'

'Did he, by Jove?' Everett asked, his chest puffing with joy. 'Mighty handsome of him to say so. Come along then, lass, if you've a mind to.' He turned aside to Lady Althea to add, 'A taking little baggage, the gel, but her brother is backward as a faun.'

'You come with Aunt, then, Gwen,' Lady Althea said.

'And you stay with Aunt Harris, Ralph,' I added, trying to suppress my rage at her stealing my title.

'I will give the old girl a quick tour and be back,' Everett said to me in a secret aside as they went out.

The three of them left, laughing and talking together, such a strangely mismated pair. Mama, Ralph, and I went for a walk through the small lime grove behind the cottage. Mrs Pudge allowed Lady to accompany us, with many injunctions to protect her, take her up in our arms, if the devil cat from the Manor should appear.

'I saw him crouched on his haunches in the rose garden, lying in wait to catch my birds. I'll take the broom to that warlock one of these days. You'd think the pail of slops would have been enough to discourage him, but no, he's back bold as brass, determined to eat them up. Does Lord Menrod never feed him?' she asked Ralph.

'He lives in the stables and catches mice,' Ralph answered.

'It's the cheese room he ought to be put in, right here at the cottage,' she advised my mother.

'Or up on the thatched roof,' I added.

There was total chaos when we went to collect Lady. She was gone, disappeared out the closed kitchen door, by the demonic powers of the black devil. A search was instigated at once; all hands, including Pudge, ourselves, and the groom, were sent out. I was the one to find the miscreants, and was foolish enough to tell Mrs Pudge what I had seen. The devil was walking toward Lady with a mouse in his mouth. He presented it proudly to her; she rejected both gift and donor with disdain. She looked at the cat as if he were a worm, then glided toward me, to be taken up in my arms.

'That bloody and deceitful cat won't live out half his days,' she stormed. 'I'll put an end to him myself, trying to lead my Lady astray. He's *wicked*, presenting his snares to her.'

'Cats will be cats, Mrs Pudge. Lady has reached the age when she is attracted to the opposite sex. There is no fighting with nature. *I* think you should bestow her hand on old Tom, and have done with it.'

'Or have her spayed,' Mama added more practically.

We finished our walk just as Everett's carriage brought the others back. Gwen was the first out. She ran to me, her eyes shining with pleasure. 'Look what Mr Everett gave me, Aunt,' she said, holding for my inspection a pretty statue of a dog, not valuable at all – it was only plaster – but attractive to a child.

'How nice. Did you say thank you, dear?'

'Of course! I'm not a child,' she answered, offended.

Lady Althea and Everett remained on excellent terms, she flirting her head off, and he his usual pleasant self. No child, she expressed her thanks very civilly.

'You haven't seen the half of it,' he told her. 'There is twice as much stuff upstairs. You'll have to come back.'

'Was the portrait one of your ancestors?' I asked, as that had been the point of the trip, to discover the fact.

'No, and not very like me either,' she answered, with a laughing glance to her host. 'I am very angry with Mr Everett. It was a woman with *gray* hair.'

'It looked red to me, the way he had the sun shining behind her. Dashed pretty anyhow, for an older malkin. As you are yourself, ma'am, if I may make so bold as to say so,' he added, with a gallant bow.

'He is incorrigible. I don't know how you put up with him.' Lady Althea laughed gaily. I would have been tempted to strike him, had he said such a thing to me, but she was more forgiving. They parted still friends. Everyone left in the greatest good mood, all promising one another we would meet again soon.

'Don't forget you are coming to see me ride tomorrow,' Ralph called as he left.

'I'll be there,' I promised. Lady Althea cast a sly glance at me, suspecting my motives in going up to the Manor, I believe, as certain amongst us suspected her reason for coming to our cottage.

Mrs Pudge, still irate over her cat, said frankly, 'The woman is casting out her snares to Mr Everett. You'd better look sharp, miss, or she'll pull him out from under your feet.'

'Feet? Surely you mean nose, Mrs Pudge.'

'You use him for a doormat. Feet is what I said, and what I meant. The only cure for it is for you to have him, marry him.'

'The cure promises to be worse than the disease.'

'Aye, the cure makes the disease look sick. As for me and Pudge, we'd rather be doorkeeper at an alms-house than to dwell at Oakdene, and so I tell you.'

'He sets a lovely table,' Mama pointed out. The Pudges eat largely and well.

'We'll not partake of his dainties, thank you very much. Wouldn't we look fine as state monkeys rigged out in a red suit sprinkled with brass buttons and gold braid?'

'He would not expect you to wear a red suit,' I pointed out, to tease her.

'Don't lead him to believe Pudge would make such a gudgeon of himself either. What does he pay, do you know?' she asked, as an afterthought.

'Plenty.'

'I don't doubt it. Money covers him like a garment. You'd have more than heart could wish if you took him. Some sly girl will snap him up fast enough. A word to the wise.'

Mama looked hopefully to see how I reacted to these varied bits of advice. 'I was never sly,' I said.

'No, nor wise either, like your sister was,' Mrs Pudge retorted, then swaggered off, her topknot sinking to the side of her head.

It is impossible not to envision how your life could be changed, when you have had an offer. Even though I had declined, and meant it, I found myself conjuring with what life would be like at Oakdene, with myself in the mistress's seat. I would indeed have more money than my simple heart could wish. Everyone thought I should accept. Menrod, Mama, even Mrs Pudge and Mr Doyle. One thing was clear after the visit;

whatever my own personal advantages, it would be unconscionable to toss Ralph into that household, where he was considered a moonling. I felt a burning resentment at Everett's treatment of him, though Gwen had managed to bring him around her thumb in a hurry. Of course Everett was out of reason fond of me, and I was quite as good a manager as Gwen, in the matter of Mr Everett.

What did he see in me? I wondered. It was Menrod who put the idea into my head. I am vainly human enough to have found it natural, but as I considered our relationship, and more particularly his taste, it *did* strike me as odd, this unrelenting passion he had for me. I had never encouraged him, not one bit. His passion was not physical, either; there were no dying glances lingering on my face or form, no extraordinary efforts to get me alone for a spot of lovemaking. It was very strange. I would have thought he would favor a grander lady than myself, someone more like Lady Althea, but his attitude to her was not loverlike. He treated her as he treated Menrod, or myself – like an equal. He never groveled or flattered, and never tried to lord it over anyone either. Really he was complicated, for a simple-seeming man.

# Chapter Thirteen

*T*he next morning, we awoke to see dull gray skies loom-ing overhead. It was poor weather for Ralph to be riding, which made me wonder whether I ought to go up to the Manor or not. I didn't want to disappoint him. By ten, it was pouring torrents, but by noon the clouds had emptied, and the sun was struggling to penetrate through the remaining wisps. Though the ground was soaked, Mama and I decided to take the short trip anyway. Menrod had used his influence to get himself an excellent metaled road to Reading, the same one we took to his place.

The butler insisted on calling Menrod to greet us. 'Don't bother to disturb him,' I said. 'It is the children we have come to see.'

'His lordship is expecting you,' he answered, and went to fetch him.

'Ralph must have told him we were coming. I did not want any to-do over the visit.'

'You told me he would not be here, Gwendolyn,' Mama complained. His few visits to our cottage had not lessened her aversion to him.

When he entered smiling a moment later, it was hard to see what she feared. He was becoming more sociable, more friendly, noticeably so.

'Good day, Menrod. I told your butler not to disturb you, but he insisted,' I said. Mama nodded.

'The occasions when I am allowed to welcome Peter's family to the Manor are too rare. I asked to be notified when you arrived. Ralph assured me you were to come, to see him perform. I feared the rain might detain you.'

'Oh, no, we are not likely to shrink up like a woolen if we get wet, but I doubt Ralph will ride today. The ground is slippery. I did not want to disappoint him, so we came anyway. We'll see him ride another time.'

'We'll give the ground half an hour to dry, then call him down.'

I could see Mama did not relish the half hour of his sole company, but I admit I was flattered at the attention.

'Any news from Culligan?' he asked.

'No, I have hired Mr Doyle in his stead.'

'From the ridiculous to the sublime, I see. Culligan is too shifty for his own good. Your taking on Doyle makes me wonder whether you are serious in your quest for the children. He is not known for his ingenuity.'

It confirmed my own opinion of the man, but I refused to change again. 'He is honest, upright. The very fact of having such a representative will do us some good.'

'His good character has not made him famous, or even known in London,' he disillusioned us. 'He deals in very small fish; one might almost say minnows. Local wills, real estate, partnerships – that sort of thing. I hobble my own chances, to tell you so. He is an excellent fellow,' he finished, brandishing his crossed fingers to show he fibbed.

Mama frowned in perplexity. I smiled, but was equally perplexed.

'I cannot offer you the variety your better friend can, but may I offer you some wine, or tea?' he asked.

'A cup of tea would be nice,' Mama answered.

'Gwen tells me she was at Oakdene yesterday,' he went on. I was surprised Gwen should be his informant, and not Lady Althea.

'Yes, she came away with a piece of plunder. Have you seen it?'

'More times than I care to. She's part horse-dealer, that one. I might as well warn you, so that you may alert Mrs Pudge, she had her eye on that pretty white kitten your housekeeper keeps at the cottage.'

'I wish her luck of getting *that!* Mrs Pudge would as lief part with the last good tooth in her head,' Mama told him.

A silence descended, which I brought to an end by relating the saga of the devil cat and Lady.

'If she's already got a litter in her, you may keep her. We have a dozen cats cluttering up the stables,' he said, with feeling.

Mama was shocked speechless at such broad talk. I said, 'If she has, it is your bounden duty to take charge of half the litter, sir. We know who is to blame if Lady is in trouble.'

'I hold the theory that ladies who get into trouble must take the blame, and the consequences, to themselves. If she behaved as she ought, she would not be in trouble.'

'You have a theory to fit every occasion. When do you find time to form them all?'

'They spring into my mind. Folks say, you know, that small minds are interested in people, medium ones in things, and great ones in theories. I seldom think of anything but theories,' he said soberly.

My mother was fairly fuming with his conceit, though if she had deigned to glance at him, she would have seen he was biting back a smile. She said scarcely a word throughout the entire half hour, which made it encumbent on me to chatter endlessly, on the most mundane of topics. After uttering every banality I could lay tongue to, I suggested the children be sent for.

'Is half an hour up so soon?' he asked, drawing out his watch. 'It seems we just sat down.'

They came pelting noisily down the stairs, Gwen in the lead. I was touched to see she carried Goldie, her mother's old rag doll. I mentioned it to her.

'I don't want to get my good one dirty,' she answered, diminishing my first rush of affection.

'Just like Hettie!' my mother exclaimed. 'She too was very careful of all her things. Unlike *you*, Gwendolyn, who never cared what damage you did to your gowns.'

'And still don't,' Menrod mentioned in a soft voice, his eyes examining the hem of my skirt, which had got splattered by the short walk to and from the carriage. 'It is a very pretty gown you have destroyed, too,' he added.

Ralph was smiling shyly in the background, waiting his turn for attention. I ignored Menrod's ill manners and had a few words with my nephew. 'Are you going to tackle a ride today, Ralph, or do you think it too wet outside?' I asked.

'Wet? Rubbish, the ground was dry hours ago,' Menrod said airily. 'Come and show your skills off to the ladies, Ralph.'

We all went out to an enclosed field, where the Menrod children have learned to ride for generations. It was grass, for easy falling, and fenced high enough that a pony could not bolt beyond the training area. A Welsh pony was brought from the stable. I expected someone would lift Ralph into the saddle, but he led Rufus to the fence, and used the lower railing for a mounting block.

'Why don't you give him a hand?' I asked Menrod when two efforts were unsuccessful.

'He's got to learn to do it for himself. He's not a lady.'

'*I* could do it,' Gwen said. 'When are you going to get *me* a pony, Uncle? I am older than Ralph. I should have got one first.'

For once, I agreed with her. She was eager to ride; Ralph was not enjoying it at all, to judge by the grim set of his jaws and the clenching of his fingers on the reins. He walked the pony around the ring twice, relaxing a little on the second trip. He was daring enough to glance at me, with a proud smile.

'Now trot him, Ralph,' Menrod called.

Ralph obediently gave his pony the signal that set him trotting. The boy's relaxation was over; he sat as stiff as a tin soldier in the saddle, while Menrod called assorted commands to him. The pony was turned to the right and left, and around in large circles.

'*I* could do it better. *I'm* not afraid,' Gwen boasted.

'Shoulders back. You're not a straw man, Ralph,' Menrod called. When Ralph remained hunched in fright, his uncle took a few steps toward him. The animal took fright, speeded up to a canter, which undid Ralph's shaky confidence entirely. He became so flustered he fell from the saddle onto the ground, scarcely missing the pony's rear hooves.

I ran forward to help him, fearful that he had broken something in the tumble. Menrod held me back. 'Leave him. He's all right.' He called to the boy, 'On your feet, Ralph. Back in the saddle.'

Ralph began to arise, slowly, unwillingly, with an appealing eye to me to rescue him.

'That's enough for today,' I said firmly. 'The ground is damp; I think the pony slipped on the wet grass.'

'The *pony* did not slip; Ralph did,' Menrod contradicted. 'No harm done. He'll have plenty of spills before he's through. Up you go, Ralph.'

Ralph, with his head down, took the reins and led the pony back to the fence, to mount once more, awkwardly, his little feet slipping and sliding on the fence rail. 'Menrod, this is cruel. Let him come in. Can't you see he's frightened half to death? He's too young to be riding. He's only four years old.'

'Closer to five. He's two years behind schedule. His father was *jumping* ponies at five.'

Ralph, with his ears perked to hear the decision, stood with his foot on the fence railing, looking at us. I read an appeal in his big dark eyes, the hope that I would save him.

'*I* could do it. Let *me* try, Uncle,' Gwen begged.

'Let Gwen have a turn,' I suggested.

'Gwen is not dressed for it. Come on, Ralph. What are you waiting for?' he asked impatiently.

My heart ached to see poor little Ralph crawl back into the saddle, stiffer than before, more hesitant, while Menrod stood, implacable. There was not an ounce of mercy, of yielding, in him. Ralph was his nephew, and he must perform to the Menrod standard, if it killed him.

Mama too made soft sounds of disapproval at the performance going forth.

'If anything happens to him, I will hold *you* responsible,' I said, my voice shrill, riding on the air.

'I wish you will stop making a mountain of a molehill. If you only came here to *discourage* Ralph, it would be better if you had not come at all,' he answered angrily.

'We are not leaving till you let him down from that brute's back!'

Ralph kept looking and listening, to learn his fate. 'Will you get on with it!' Menrod shouted. My nephew had no choice but to continue the lesson, which had become a lesson in inhumanity. The child was trembling with fright. I waited with Mama just outside the training ring till it was over. It went on for half an hour longer. At the end of that time, I congratulated Ralph, then told Menrod we must leave immediately for home.

'You see I was right,' he boasted. 'Ralph can do it. He does not want too much mothering, or he'll turn into a full-fledged sissy. He needs a firm hand.'

Ralph was beyond hearing, leading his pony back to the stable. He looked so small, so vulnerable, I wanted to run after him and kidnap him away to the cottage. My control broke. I turned on Menrod in a frenzy.

'He is not the only one here who wants a firm hand. It is unconscionable of you to force him to ride at his age, and in this weather. It is a lucky thing for you he was not maimed, or killed. I shall speak to Mr Doyle about this, and see if he can't get an injunction to stop you.'

'Miss Harris, don't make a flaming jackass of yourself,' was his answer.

'Come, Mama. We are leaving now. Good day to you. Goodbye, Gwen.'

We strode off to the front of the house, then had to stand five minutes, waiting till our carriage was sent around. Menrod did not have the common courtesy to accompany us, but went to the stable to bully Ralph some more.

As a consequence of the visit, our ameliorating relationship with Menrod took a turn for the worse. Doyle was perfectly useless to us. He rambled on about motives and so on, in the affair of the riding lesson. Naturally I could not accuse Menrod outright of trying to kill the boy. It was his insensitivity that was in question, his harshness to a minor in his keeping. Was the animal vicious? Doyle asked, and such stupid questions as that. Finally he decreed that learning to ride was a fit pastime for a child of four, providing that due precautions were taken for his safety. Forcing him to remount an animal who had just thrown him, when he was trembling with fright, was no dereliction of duty, it seemed, providing it was done by Lord Menrod.

Mrs Pudge, always ready to incline her ear to the wrongdoings of old devil's owner, declared that a brutish man knoweth not, and if the Lord in His heaven had His wits about Him, the heathen would perish like the beasts.

'Just when I was beginning to think he was reasonable, too,' I fretted.

'Reasonable?' Mama asked, gazing at the enclosed staircase. 'No, he was never reasonable, Gwendolyn, but only conning us, to make us give up on the children.'

'Aye, using words smoother than butter and softer than oil, to con you along,' Mrs Pudge said knowingly, 'as that black cat did to my Lady. I don't like the size of her. She's walking at an odd gait lately. I do believe she's increasing. If she is, I'll disown her, put the daughter of wickedness out from my roof.'

We suffered a spell of bad weather, drizzle that continued for two days instead of working itself into a good downpour to clear the air. It kept callers away, but at least it would keep Ralph from being forced into more lessons, so my mind was easy on that score.

During a respite of the drizzle on the second evening, Mr Everett came to call, and was told the story of the riding lesson by Mama.

'I have to agree with Menrod,' he said when it was done.

'If you had been there to see him, you would not agree,' Mama said sadly. 'The poor wee tyke, shaking in his boots. 'Twas enough to break your heart.'

'It's common knowledge that the only thing to do after a tumble is to remount at once, or you'll never do it. The fear goes on growing, the longer you put it off, till in the end it is too big to get over.'

'You forget the ground was wet,' I told him.

'Menrod is a man of sound judgment. He'd not have allowed it if he felt it was dangerous. Those slow-witted lads like young Ralph will often surprise you by being good at sports.'

As Mr Everett was being more bovine than usual, we soon spoke of other things – a new railing being installed around the upper landing of Oakdene, something with larger, more ornate spindles than those presently in place, at a cost of seventy-eight pounds and nine shillings. Much later in the visit, he asked, 'Have you got your tickets to Lady Menrod's ball yet?'

'No, we have not. Has she sent them out already?' I asked, thinking Everett must have heard the story in town.

'I don't know that she has. She dropped mine off at the house in person yesterday.'

He related this amazing item with the nonchalance of a socialite. A call from Lady Menrod on Mr Everett sent my head reeling. What could account for it? 'I did not realize you knew her,' Mama said, showing all the incredulity I felt.

'I didn't, before the call. It was Lady Althea who brought her, to see the picture, you know, that resembles herself. *I* think it does, at least. They both roasted me for saying so, but the eyes and nose are very like, and the full, plump figure.'

'You must have been surprised to see them at your door,' Mama said.

'I was. I asked Lady Althea to come back sometime and see the other pictures, but didn't half expect she would do it. They took a longish tour through all the rooms, up and down. I think they had been bored to flinders at home, with all the rain. In the end I had to invite them to take luncheon with me. It was no bother, for there is always good food in the house, and I was not going out anywhere.'

'They were eager to see it, having the horses put to in that downpour,' Mama said. She was not happy at the visit. She discerned a scheme to rob me of my beau.

'It surprised me,' he repeated, 'but not so much as being asked back to call on them. I am to take tea there tomorrow. Are yourselves included in the party?'

'No, we are not,' I answered, feeling my first niggle of pique – not jealousy, but pique.

'I came to offer you a lift, if you were.'

'Is it to be a large party?' I enquired, with very real curiosity. I did not think Lady Menrod would include Everett in a large party of her friends, yet to invite him to a small party was more flattering.

'I've no idea. I'll let you know after it is over, if you are curious. The ladies like to keep abreast of all the gossip, I know.'

I had not thought to see the day when I had to learn my gossip from a lumber merchant!

He did not remain long. There was no change in his attitude to me, no reason to believe Lady Althea was chasing him or that he was beginning to return the attention to her. It was one of those social oddities that occur in the country, when company is thin and time hanging heavy on everyone's hands. The ladies had been bored, and gone to pass a day in ogling Oakdene. They were nice enough to return his hospitality. That was all, and to go on threatening me that I was 'losing' a parti in whom I had no real interest was absurd of Mama, and annoying after ten or twelve repetitions. It was enough to put me in a pet, along with the dreary weather and hearing nothing about Gwen and Ralph. The visit had an effect on Mama's interest in the ball. From wondering how she could avoid it, she now was impatient to receive her card.

# Chapter Fourteen

*I*t began to seem, after a few days, that we were not going to receive invitations to the ball at all. Several neighbors mentioned having got theirs, while we nodded and implied we would see them there, unable to credit we were being cut. It was surely an oversight. Mrs Tighe actually brought her card with her. I glanced at it, to see it signed by Lady Menrod. I had nothing against the dowager countess, nor she against me. She would not have left me off her list unless she had been asked to do so by someone close to her. We had not seen Menrod nor heard from him since the day of the riding lesson. It was hard to believe he would be so petty as to exclude us, but impossible not to wonder.

He had sent the children down once with a servant. They came rather late in the afternoon, with orders that they be home for tea. He did not bother to enquire first whether the hour for the visit was convenient. We happened to be having a game of whist with a few neighbors at the time, but I was able to get free from the table. We usually invite four, which brings the total of ladies to six, so that we may each have a turn free to gossip.

I was anxious to hear about Ralph's riding. It was the first thing I asked him – how his lessons were going on. 'I don't fall any more,' he assured me.

'Uncle Menrod got me a pony, too,' Gwen said happily. 'We

both ride together now.'

'That's nice, dear.'

'I want him to take me back to London, but he won't,' she continued. 'We had a good time in London. Will you take me, Aunt?'

'I don't have a house in London, Gwen. I seldom go there.'

'You must go sometimes.'

'Once in a while, to put up at a hotel.'

'I would love to stay at a hotel,' she said, smiling fondly. She really is a pretty rogue. 'I have never stayed at one. Will you take me, the next time you go?'

'If it is possible, I'll take you both.'

'When?' she demanded.

'When I can. I am not planning a trip soon.'

'Then will you take us to Reading, at least? I have to have a new riding habit.'

'I can do that tomorrow, if it is convenient for you. I have to do some shopping myself.'

'I'll ask Uncle if we may go.'

'Can I come too?' Ralph was not tardy to ask.

'Of course, goose! You didn't think the carriage would leave without you, I hope.'

'What will you buy for Ralph?' Gwen asked.

'An iced cone. How would you like that?'

'If you are buying me a bonnet and riding habit, you'll have to get Ralph more than ice,' she pointed out reasonably.

I had not realized I was to buy the riding habit. I thought I would select it, while Menrod paid, but the sly puss had outwitted me. It would look too skintish to refuse, when she had taken it for an offer. I could not afford to alienate her at this time, when I wanted them in my custody.

'We'll think of something,' I said vaguely. What I thought was that Menrod might prohibit the trip. I would not resent it in the least, as my purse was so close to empty, after hiring two lawyers in two weeks.

Gwen was made much of by our visitors. She was pretty, elegant, not shy to put herself forward. She would coast through life, making friends easily, and using them if they did not look sharp. Ralph was largely ignored, which suited his retiring nature to a T. He was uncomfortable when a few of the ladies tried to talk to him, answering in monosyllables if he could screw himself up to an answer at all.

Their visit lasted one hour exactly. The servant had waited in the kitchen with Mrs Pudge, who came to tell me the wee ones had to go now. I hoped I might hear something from the servant about the party readying at the Manor, though I would not submit him to a hard quiz, so I took Ralph and Gwen downstairs myself.

'I expect you are all in a tizzy with this ball to prepare, eh, Haskins?' I asked the footman, while Gwen slipped around behind me to speak to Mrs Pudge.

'Yes, miss,' was all he said. 'Your uncle said not to eat before you got home, Miss Gwendolyn,' he called to the minx. She had coaxed an apple tart from Mrs Pudge, who was putty in her hands. Hettie had always been a prime love of both the Pudges.

'May I please, Aunt, just one tiny little tart?' she asked, then with a laugh stuck the whole thing into her mouth. Mrs Pudge makes a special dainty tart only an inch and a half in diameter, so this was not so gross an exhibition as it sounds.

'Run along with you, baggage,' I said; then, as Ralph was looking gypped, I sneaked one into his waiting fingers as well. It disappeared in the same fashion, in one bite.

'That girl is a caution,' Haskins said, wagging his head and smiling fondly.

'Don't tell Uncle,' Gwen said, with one of her sweet smiles.

'I may forget what I saw, if you hurry up,' he agreed.

'I would like another,' Ralph announced through a mouthful of crumbs.

'Take them home before they have demolished the plate. There won't be any left for our guests,' I told Haskins.

'What time will you call for us tomorrow, Aunt, to go to Reading?' Gwen asked, before leaving.

'Why do you not have Haskins bring you here in the morning? Come early, about nine. The shops are not so busy then.'

'We have to be back to ride at two,' she pointed out.

'You are on a strict timetable, I see.'

'Yes, Uncle Menrod has a theory about it,' she said.

'I'm sure he has. See you at nine.'

They left, while I helped Mrs Pudge take the trays up to the sitting room.

Our trip to Reading went off next morning without a hitch. Haskins had the children at the door at nine sharp. 'His lordship would like them home for tea,' was the word sent down from the Manor. The timetable theory was flexible enough to allow some bending. I was happy to hear it was not lunch that was the deadline, or it would have been a scrambling expedition to town. My mother elected to stay at home, in the hope, I believe, of receiving the invitation to the ball in the mail. She was gearing up for quite a fit of the vapors over our being omitted. It was my own plan to ignore it, say nothing, even if I met Lady Menrod or her stepson in town.

We did not meet either of them. Gwen was every bit as finicky as her mother in selecting material for the new habit, and later in choosing a bonnet to suit it. Being so young, she was less aware of prices than Hettie. I suggested green, to set off her gray eyes, or even red, as she was youthful enough to look well in it. She chose blue. I had hoped to eke some small token for Ralph out of my monies, but as Gwen insisted her riding bonnet required a dashing feather, Ralph was lucky to get his iced cone.

'Let us have lunch at a hotel,' Gwen suggested.

I bribed her out of this expensive idea by listing the menu Mrs Pudge had waiting at home. I measured her up for the habit before she left. 'You will be in the highest kick of fashion once this is done,' I told her.

'May I have pleats in the skirt?' she asked.

'A flared skirt is more flattering. Pleats are bulky, especially with a jacket over them.'

'Silver buttons, then?' she haggled.

'Why not? I have a set from an old habit of my own. You are welcome to them.'

'Isn't it exciting to have new gowns?' she asked. 'And you are so good at fashions too, Aunt. Even Lady Althea agreed your green morning gown was pretty.'

'I am flattered to hear it. Agreed with whom?' I asked, wondering if it were possible Menrod had uttered a word in its praise.

'With me,' she replied. 'You always look so nice.'

I enjoyed the outing tremendously. It was like being a mother, to have the children along with me, driving, going through the shops, and later preparing the habit. Gwen could be charming, when she took into her head to be. As she grew up, it would be fun to outfit her, and take her around to parties. Ralph, my favorite, was not overlooked either, though he played second fiddle on that occasion. When we were done, I noticed he had wandered off from the room, to seek amusement outdoors.

I went after him, and found him pushing himself back and forth on an old swing that has hung from one of the lime trees out back forever. It had served the inhabitants of the cottage for eons, and even myself, once or twice when no one was around to watch me. He had to hang off the edge of the seat to get his short legs to the ground to push himself.

'Hold on tight, I'll push you,' I offered, but was careful not to push too hard.

'Push me higher,' he urged, being more daring that I would have thought.

I pushed till his toes were not far from hitting the lower boughs when he reached the top of the arc. Squeals of delight accompanied each rise. We were so engrossed in the game, we did not see Menrod approaching from behind.

'Can this possibly be the cautious Miss Harris, indulging Ralph in such a dangerous activity?' he asked.

'Dangerous? It is not in the least dangerous. He is enjoying it,' I answered. His shouts showed clearly it was the case.

'If he should tumble, he will fall farther than he did from the pony's back.'

I eased off on my pushing, let him subside to a gentle sway. 'Is it teatime so soon? The children were about to go to you, but Ralph wanted a swing before he left.' I expected some show of ill temper from Menrod, after our last unpleasant encounter. There was no evidence of it. His manner was closer to conciliating.

'There is no hurry. I was passing by and decided to pick them up, to save a trip. Did you ladies get yourselves outfitted for the new gowns?' he asked.

'It was only Gwen who was to get material, for her new riding habit, you know. Now that you have got her a pony, she will need a habit.'

'Another habit?' he asked.

'*Another?* I thought she didn't have one.'

'She would have me believe she had outgrown the new one she got before leaving India, but it looked fine to me. It was kind of you to indulge her.'

'Not at all. It was a pleasure,' I answered, angry as a hornet at being duped by the girl.

'Are you not having a new gown yourself, for the ball next week?' he asked.

'Your ball, you mean?' I verified, rather surprised at the question.

'No, Lady Menrod's ball for her cousin, to be held at my house.'

'I shan't require a new gown for that,' I answered stiffly.

'Palming us off with an old one, eh? I don't think we are to take that as a compliment.'

'As a matter of fact, I shan't be wearing a ball gown that night at all. We are not attending the ball.'

He stiffened up, adopting an offended face. 'No doubt there is a reason for it?' he asked.

'The best reason in the world. We were not invited.'

He was very much taken aback. A frown formed between his eyes. Within an instant, it vanished, and a new expression was put on, a very conning expression. 'Don't tell me I forgot to mail your invitations!' he exclaimed, rather loudly.

'I don't know whether it was an oversight or an intentional omission, but we did not receive cards from your stepmother. We are hardly the best of friends, however. We did not take it amiss, I assure you.'

'Don't be foolish. Of course you are invited. The whole neighborhood is coming. They have even sent a card to Mr Everett. I – I told Lady Menrod I would like to invite a few of my own particular friends, send the cards out myself. I believe I may have mentioned your name in with the others. That explains it. I shall send them out this very day.'

He was a poor liar, but a fast thinker to make up for it. We had been omitted, for what reason I do not know, unless the ladies thought we would attend on Mr Everett's card. That was the only thought I could think of. I accepted his story at its face value, and told him we would be happy to receive the invitations.

He hastened on to a less prickly topic. 'Ralph is making good headway with his riding lessons. It would have been poor policy to make too much of his spill. I have a theory that the only way to proceed is to remount immediately after a fall, before the fear has time to grow out of proportion.'

'I have discovered something you have in common with Mr Everett at last. He told me the same thing. *I* have a theory too, that till a boy's feet reach the stirrups, he ought not to be made to ride.'

'He was not *made* to ride. *He* suggested it. It was surely not necessary for you to complain to Everett about a family matter.'

'It was mentioned in passing – by my mother, actually.'

'She must be on better terms with him than she is with me. I have noticed she seldom utters a word, if she can help it. Does she dislike me so much?' he asked bluntly.

'She never said so, if she does. I believe you said something nasty to her at the time of Hettie's marriage to Peter. I don't know what it was, but she has said more than once you cut up stiff over it.'

He rubbed his chin, in an effort to retrace that ancient conversation. He soon shrugged his shoulders and dismissed it. 'I was not particularly pleased at the match. The family felt Peter, as the younger son, ought to have looked out for some well-dowered lady. I did not *forbid* the match, as I could have done.'

'Why did you not?'

'He told me he couldn't live without her – romantics are allowed such exaggerations in the throes of love. Of course even he did not mean it literally, but he convinced me that for him, life would not be worth living without her, so I reluctantly gave them my blessing.'

Ralph's swing slowed to a stop. He jumped down and came to us. 'Why don't you run inside and call your sister?' Menrod suggested.

'Will you come in?' I asked, for politeness's sake.

'Let us wait here, the weather is so fine. Do you want a push while we wait?' he asked, indicating the swing. The suggestion surprised me, such a quaint notion, to spring from Menrod's worldly head.

'No, but I shall take advantage of the seat. I am tired from shopping all morning.'

I arranged my skirts carefully around me, not entirely unconscious of the picture I made. The lime orchard is the prettiest feature of our landscape here at the cottage. The roses that climb over the cottage front, once an item of great beauty, do not flourish as they did in days of yore, though they are pretty for about a week in early June. I was a trifle put out to see Menrod stroll away from me, behind, where he would see nothing but my back. Soon I realized he had gone around to push me in the swing, despite my declining his offer. He began at first with a gentle pressure, just moving the swing a foot back and forth. It was too foolish to object to this, so I said nothing. The pushes increased in force, till I was sailing through the air, my skirts ballooning around me.

'That's high enough, Menrod,' I ordered. 'Stop now, please.'

He pushed harder, harder, till I actually had some fears for my safety. On the swing forward, my toes disappeared in the leaves of the tree. My protests too rose higher, till I was shrieking like a fishwife, holding on for dear life to the cords between my fingers. I could feel my hair slipping away from its pins, and was helpless to get it under control. My skirts were blowing straight into my face, causing a disgraceful show below. Then, when I was distracted with fear and embarrassment, *then* he strolled around to the front to observe me. As the momentum decreased, and I settled down to a still high but no longer dangerous arc, I was able to see the expression on his face. He looked demonic, with a satyrical smile on his lips and laughter in his eyes. I was so angry I leapt off before the swing was anywhere near stopping. My precipitous flight from the seat sent me catapulting forward, where I stubbed my toe and would have hit the ground, had he not had the presence of mind to catch me. His hands grasped my upper arms tightly, while my head bumped against his chest. I was gasping for breath.

'Why in the devil did you do that?' I demanded angrily.

He held me back to examine me. With his head perched on one side, he answered, 'Curiosity,' in a reasonable tone.

'Next time you want to test some theory about motion, please submit someone else to the experiment.'

'Oh, it wasn't a theory of motion I was testing. Let us say, rather, it was emotion.'

'If your aim was to see how angry you could make me, then let me tell you. . . .'

'Angry enough to put a sparkle in your eyes and a blush on your cheeks, at least, which is an improvement over your customary composure.'

'Thank you,' I sniffed, in an attempt at satire.

Gwen and Ralph had come running up during the fracas. 'Why are you holding Aunt Harris, Uncle?' Gwen enquired, in a clear, piping voice.

'To prevent her from scratching my eyes out,' he answered.

I wrenched free from his hold. 'Your uncle is in a playful mood today, children,' I explained.

'Not at all,' he contradicted. 'I was conducting an experiment.'

'What did you find out?' she asked, with a curious look from one of us to the other.

'I merely confirmed that your aunt has a temper. You interrupted us before we were through,' he answered, with a soft smile curving his lips. His eyes regarded my face for a long moment, then he tucked a stray lock of my hair behind my ear.

'It looks better in disorder, but less like Miss Harris. These tokens of abandonment

*Do more bewitch me, than when art*
*Is too precise in every part.*

Why don't we try it *à la victime* for the ball?'

He bowed and left before I thought of a retort to this brash speech. 'Come along, urchins,' he called over his shoulder to the children. 'And say thank you to your Aunt. We must not forget our manners.'

The children obeyed, but Menrod so far forgot his manners as to leave without apologizing.

# Chapter Fifteen

We had two minor excitements the next morning. The noisier of the two by far was the disappearance of Lady. She had been restless of late, due to her maturing state. In theory she was restricted in the house to the kitchen and Mrs Pudge's chamber, but in fact it was not unusual to see her parade through the place, upstairs and down, as if she owned it. When Mrs Pudge came asking whether we had seen her, I suggested she try the bedrooms.

'I believe she hears the mice in the thatched roof, and sits on the bed, wondering how to get at them,' I mentioned.

'She might be out back, trying to get at the roof from a tree,' Mama suggested.

Our housekeeper flapped off to check out this possibility. Around ten, she came back to ask if we had seen Lady. 'She's not had her breakfast. She never goes off without her breakfast. She was curled up on the end of my bed last night, and this morning when I got up, she was gone. Pudge left the door ajar.'

'She could not have left the house, though,' Mama pointed out.

'Pudge is as blind as a bat. He was out early this morning, getting fuel for my stove. She walked right past him, though he won't admit it. If there's nothing special you want me for, I'm going to take a walk around the orchard. She must be starved by now.'

While she was gone, our second excitement occurred. With Mrs Pudge out hunting Lady, and her husband in the kitchen doing her work, I was consigned to the role of butler. My first admission was Lord Menrod and the children. His excuse for coming was to allow Gwen to show off her new pony, and Ralph his improved skill in the saddle. I noticed my niece was outfitted in an elegant green riding habit, by no means too small for her. The minx had got me to provide her a new one, when her own was better than mine. I do not often get to ride, but occasionally a neighbor's mount is put at my disposal.

'Will you come out and watch us ride, Grandma?' Gwen asked.

We were happy to go, especially on a fresh morning in April when spring was just arrived. Gwen would be a fine horse-woman in a few years. She had a good seat, an easy hand, and no fear of her mount. Menrod proudly proclaimed her a 'natural,' while I loudly praised Ralph's scanty progress. It was a pity the boy of the family could not be the athlete. They rode in circles around the family garden, then were allowed to trot down through the orchard. With nothing but Menrod's company to amuse her, Mama soon found the wind was rising, and went indoors.

'You will stay out and watch the children, Gwendolyn?' she asked.

'We'll stay, Mrs Harris,' Menrod answered quickly.

'Do you want another turn on the swing?' he asked with a bantering smile, setting off at a slow pace toward the orchard, following the children.

'I am not dressed for it,' I answered. 'Trousers ought to be worn by any damsel foolish enough to let you push her.'

'Here I had hopes you referred only to a lack of lace on your petticoats. I do believe ladies in swings ought to be plentifully supplied with lace on their undergarments – "tempestuous petticoats," the poet calls them. It is an international thing – you see it in the Watteau paintings Everett has as well. You favor a spartan toilette, Miss Harris.'

'If I ever pose for Watteau, I shall be sure to load myself down with lace.'

'That is unlikely. The man has been dead for close to a hundred years. You are not much interested in art, I take it?'

'No, not much,' I replied, scanning the grass for Lady.

'Do you ride at all?' was his next question.

'I used to, a few years ago. My mount expired of old age, and I have not ridden since.'

'You must have had some lively jogs, those last few years. Why do you not get a new mount?'

'For lack of interest. And capital,' I added, more truthfully.

'How delightful to find you capable of a pun.'

'Equally surprising to find you appreciate one,' I replied, with matching condescension.

'Have I offended again? Tch tch, and I wasn't even trying.'

I veered off to the left to look behind a thorn bush, thinking Lady might be lurking there to catch a bird.

'Are we looking for something?' he asked.

'You might keep your eyes peeled for Lady, Mrs Pudge's white kitten. She has vanished into thin air.'

'How intriguing. The Lady Vanishes – quite like a gothic mystery. I expect you read gothic stories.'

'I haven't time for much reading. She does not have wings, Menrod. The ground is where we will find her,' I said, as he had stopped to stare all around – up in the trees, the sky, and other unlikely places.

'I was admiring the newly formed leaves, so dainty this time of year, like green lace.'

'That would appeal to you, of course. You have a fetish about lace. Were you deprived of it as a child?'

'As a child, but I have made up the deficiency since coming of age,' he answered daringly, with a bold smile to show he spoke of petticoat dealings.

I did not humor him with a sniff, or show any sign of being either outraged or impressed with his boasting. He decided to give me an explanation. 'I feel one owes it to himself to enjoy and appreciate all the good things the Lord has provided us with on this earth: pretty women, the arts, literature, music, horses, and so on. It is a mistake to think goodness exists in denial of the bounty around us, don't you agree?'

'This is another of the famous Menrod theories, I assume. Enjoy them, by all means, if you are able to afford it. I enjoy what meager bounties as come my way. The trouble with theories is trying to execute them. I'm sure a veteran theoretician like yourself has discovered that fact eons ago.'

'Money and freedom of one's time are of course necessary to appreciate the finer things of life. If you accepted Everett's offer, you would have both.'

'I would also have Everett. Tell me, Menrod, are the children included in your list of the good things of life to be enjoyed? Are they considered as paintings, or horses, in your scheme of things? Interesting objects, and no more?'

We had caught up with them. They *did* make a lovely picture, the two youngsters on their matching ponies, trotting and laughing in the sunlight. As I glanced at Menrod, I noticed the appreciative smile he wore at the handsome picture.

'More than that, though they ought to be painted. Who should we have do it?' He gave a disparaging laugh. 'You would not know the good artists working in England, of course. Reynolds and Romney are gone.'

'This sounds a project to please yourself, not the children.'

'I shall teach them to appreciate the finer things in life. Can *you*, in your straitened circumstances?'

'So there *was* a point to this conversation! I began to think you were drawing forth my deficiencies for no other reason than meanness.'

His smile vanished, to be replaced by a black scowl. 'It is not wealth that creates a mean mind, but poverty,' he answered sharply.

'Sorry I cannot afford to be so magnanimous as you.'

'You cannot afford to raise the children as they ought to be raised, and you will not accept Everett to make it possible. You are not willing to sacrifice for them. What makes you think you deserve them more than I?'

'What sacrifice are you willing to make?'

'I am here. Normally I would be elsewhere in the spring, having a better time. That shows clearly I am willing to sacrifice for them.'

'Is it such a sacrifice, to spend six weeks in a mansion, surrounded by every luxury money can buy? All things are relative.'

He soon found it expedient to take the children home, mentioning in an offhand way he wished to arrange to have their portraits taken.

One excitement that did not visit us was the invitations to the ball. We now knew we were to attend, but it would have been more graceful if we had a piece of cardboard saying so. I, for one, was uncertain whether we should go without receiving the invitations. A dozen times a day Mama bemoaned their absence.

'Menrod must have forgotten to tell his stepmother,' she would fret.

'He said he would post them himself,' I reminded her.

'It has slipped his mind. How very odd.'

Mr Everett dropped in every second day, as usual. He

occasionally teased me about our spurious engagement, but in no pressing way. He mentioned having seen Lady Althea, Menrod, and the children in Reading on two different occasions. 'A fine-looking family,' he commented. 'I believe it may come to a match ere long. Don't fret your pretty little head, Gwendolyn. Lady Althea will make them a good mother. She is very fond of those kiddies, treats them as if they were her own.' I made some ill-natured remark that set Mama to tsking at me.

Lady did not show up, throwing Mrs Pudge into a great pelter. She spoke of the loss till we were all weary with her groaning. She was consumed with grief, as though it were a daughter that had gone, and not a stupid cat.

'That devil cat has got her,' she repined. 'Kidnapped her, taken her away to the Manor. She made her bed in hell, and must lie on it.'

Ralph and Gwen came down twice, on those days when Mr Everett did not come. Gwen came to follow the progress of her riding habit, and to urge even greater fineries on me. 'Could I have a little mink collar on it, Aunt?' she asked sweetly. 'I shall keep it for a winter habit. My green one will be for warmer weather, for it was made in India, you know, and is not at all heavy.'

'Children don't need fur trim, Gwen,' I told her.

'Uncle Menrod is getting me a fur-lined cape for winter,' she announced on the second call. 'I told him how *cold* I am all the time, after living in India. I think I have got a cold. My lungs are congested,' she said, with a cough to prove the point. There were other extravagant gifts from Menrod as well, more than a child required, or than were good for her. She wore a small pearl ring too, a gift from Aunt Althea for helping her wind her woolens.

Ralph was his usual undemanding self, wanting nothing but my companionship. I seem always to be pointing out Gwen's greedy side, but between asking for things, she was sweet and likable. She would be happy to curl up beside us in the sitting room and hear stories about her mother's childhood. She asked questions about it, showing how often Hettie had spoken of us, and how well she had listened too. I did not dislike her by any means, but was aware that she had a greedy streak in her makeup, or perhaps only a love of beautiful things.

One day she went to Hettie's room and picked up half a dozen of her mother's items, some books, a little wooden jewelry box with some childish beads in it, and other baubles. Mama smiled dotingly, thinking it a sentimental gesture, but it struck me as more. She had inherited this appreciation of the world's bounties from her papa's side of the family. She even tried her hand at relieving me of one of my more cherished possessions – an ivory miniature of Hettie – but I refused to let it go.

'Maybe I can get a copy made when we go to London. When are you going to take us to London, Aunt?'

'I don't plan a trip soon,' I told her stiffly.

On the fifth day after his last visit, Menrod came again, rather late in the evening. I was surprised to see him, as a hard wind had blown up, carrying with it a few drops of rain, which augured more to follow soon. The air was oppressive. We sat shivering in the sitting room, bundled in shawls, discussing the wisdom of lighting the fire and being smoked to death, but had not come to a decision.

'A terrible night,' Menrod complained, coming in to shake the rain drops from his shoulders.

'What brings you out on such a night?' Mama enquired.

'Necessity, ma'am,' he said, handing her two white squares. 'I discovered these cards under a pile of letters on my desk, and realized I had not given them to your daughter on my last visit, as I intended. I blame the lapse on her scintillating conversation.

We got pulling some crow or other, and it slipped my mind. *Very* remiss of me, but it is a formality only. You knew you were to come.'

Mama was so relieved to get the cards that she actually cropped out into a smile and a few words of gratitude.

'You need not have come out in the rain only for that,' I told him.

'You are welcome too, Miss Harris,' he answered, with a formal bow and a less formal scowl.

After a few questioning looks at the cold grate, all ready to be lit, Mama understood he was wondering why we had no fire, and suggested lighting it.

'A very good idea,' he agreed unhesitatingly.

Pudge was called, to labor with the tinder box, then with twigs, newspapers, and other inducements to the flame when the fire did not take. At length, a weak lick of orange was flickering. Menrod arose and poked about at it impatiently, rearranging the logs to allow some draught. His reward was a blast of smoke in the face that set him to coughing. On his next poke, the handle fell off the poker. He was so unaccustomed to making a fire that he picked up the hot shaft, and burned his fingers. He looked in disgruntlement at the antique fire irons. 'Does nothing work around here?' he asked in vexation.

'We like to keep the proper antiques on hand, to match the authenticity of the place,' I reminded him. Mama, still happy with the invitations, darted to the corner to retrieve the newer poker for his use. The smoke increased with the flames, till it was necessary to vacate the room or be suffocated.

'You ought to have that chimney swept out,' he informed us.

'It is the thatched roof that makes it so difficult. A man dare not stand on it, you know, and our grate is so small a boy cannot get up from below. As you mentioned yourself on the stairway when you bumped your head, people must have been smaller two hundred years ago,' I said.

'It is not at all impossible to walk on a thatched roof, providing it is done carefully,' he answered unhesitatingly.

'Pudge is not agile,' Mama apologized.

'I'll send a man down from the Manor. This is ridiculous. Where do you customarily sit when the sitting room is full of smoke?' he asked. I made sure he would leave instead, but it was not his intention.

'Gwendolyn takes refuge in her conservatory, and I go to my bed,' Mama answered.

'We shall all go to the conservatory. Bring some lights, Pudge,' Menrod ordered. 'It is as dark as pitch in this hallway,' he pointed out. A coat of light-yellow paint would lighten it, but it was only our own furnishings we dared put the brush to. As Mama was included in the command, she came along with us, still clutching the invitations.

My tiny conservatory had only two chairs, so that Pudge was required to make more than one trip. On his second, I further disobliged him by requesting some tea, which Mrs Pudge brought about twenty minutes later. She does not usually loiter when we have such high company as Menrod, but on this occasion she hovered at the door after the tea was brought.

'Excuse me, milord, but I have a troublesome matter on my mind, and want your opinion,' she said shyly.

'What is it?' he asked, startled at her behavior.

'It's my kitten,' she said, close to tears. 'The dear thing has disappeared, and I was wondering if you'd seen ought of her around your barns. A snow-white kitten, with soft and shiny fur.'

'The place is full of cats. I'll ask them tomorrow,' he said, then turned away from her. She curtsied three or four times, and backed from the doorway. 'If Lady is not there, I'll be happy to give her a replacement,' he offered.

'There would be no replacing Lady,' I told him. 'Don't think to unload your excess of strays by that ruse, unless you have a snow-white kitten.'

'A symbolic thing, is it, the white fur denoting her chaste condition? I doubt she'll be entitled to it by the time she comes home, dragging her tail behind her, and a litter as well, if I know anything.'

He looked around the room. 'I see the plants thrive, as usual. They have no aversion to their antique surroundings.'

'Gwen takes great care of them. She is puttering here half the time. If she took as much care of herself as she does of these plants, she would be better employed,' Mama told him.

'Yet they contrive to look natural, growing with wild profusion and abandonment,' he mentioned, his gaze moving around the wall. 'A certain sweet disorder that is more beguiling than formality. Everyone requires an avocation. If a lady is not interested in art, music, literature, and so on, then she is fortunate to have found something to pass her idle hours. I daresay there is as much to be learned from Nature as from books. More, according to Mr Wordsworth. You don't actually have many blooms, do you?' he asked, searching the greenery for flowers.

'I favor pure greenery – ivies of various types, and so on.'

'Why, Gwen, you have said a dozen times you would love to try your hand at orchids,' Mama corrected me.

'The plainness of your horticulture suits you,' Menrod said, comparing me to my plants. 'No showy blooms, no lacy finery, just good English stock.'

'They are free, you know,' Mama rambled on, now that she was overcoming her fear of Menrod. 'She digs up things that are growing outdoors, puts them in pots, where they thrive prodigiously. Her bedroom is the same. She has a *tree* growing in a corner, a real live tree.'

'A palm?' Menrod asked, with some interest.

'No, a lemon tree that she grew from seeds herself as an experiment.'

'It will not bear fruit if it is not grafted or fertilized,' he instructed.

'I don't expect it to. I like the leaves, the look of the tree in my room.'

'Lemon seems a suitable plant,' he said cryptically, but I understood it as a hint at my astringent nature.

'Gwendolyn could make a sow's ear of a silken purse,' Mama confided. 'She has no taste for ornament. She *removed* the silken rose from her new bonnet two years ago, saying red was too garish. Not like her sister, Hettie. She was always fond of pretty things, like little Gwen.'

'I am surprised your austerity permits you to have so many yellow furnishings,' he said, in a quizzical spirit.

'That is so we will not be bumping into them in the dark,' Mama outlined. 'The light yellow stands out in the gloom better than old oak or mahogany.'

'You actually painted good oaken and mahogany furnishings yellow?' he asked, staring at the desecration.

'No, not *good* pieces,' Mama went on to exculpate us. 'The manse we were used to live in was furnished, you see, so when we moved here, we had to *buy* our household. Most of it we picked up at Mrs Perkins's estate sale for an old song – wretched stuff, but it looks bright, at least, now.'

'Have the children begun to sit for the portraits yet?' I asked, to stem Mama's loquacity.

'Yes, and are mighty bored with it already. I think Gwendolyn is just what Mr Everett needs to tone him down, don't you, Mrs Harris?' he said, reverting quickly to the less pleasant subject.

'I have told her so a dozen times,' she answered eagerly. 'We could tame his taste, between the two of us. He is always agreeable to any hint.' This subject, in various forms, made up the last ten minutes of the visit.

When Menrod said in a reluctant way that he supposed he ought to be getting home, I hopped swiftly to my feet to see him out. 'You will want to get to the Manor before the storm breaks,' I encouraged.

'As long as I am safely out the door before you start ranting, I shall be satisfied,' he replied, with a knowing smile.

'I referred to the weather.'

'I misunderstood, but a storm is brewing inside too, I think. I was only funning. When I finally struck on a topic so agreeable to your mother, I milked it for all its worth. She is overcoming her shyness of me. I had not realized she favored the match so strongly. It must be unpleasant for you to go against her wishes – such a dutiful little daughter as you are in all other respects.'

'Don't measure me up for a halo. I am not particularly dutiful.'

'Don't disillusion me just when I feel I am beginning to understand you.'

'I didn't realize I presented such a riddle.'

'Say problem, rather. What I mean by that is, I am coming reluctantly to the conclusion you would be good for Gwendolyn. Ralph definitely needs a man's influence, but Gwen . . . she is such a conning rascal, she needs a firm hand, preferably a feminine hand. She makes cake of us men, with her feminine guile. I have actually – I can't believe I am such a soft touch – promised her a fur-lined cape for next winter. You, I know, are proof against her wheedling. She speaks often of some miniature of Hettie I am to get copied for her, as you are too mean to give her the picture of her own dear mama. I admire your powers in having withstood her persuasions.'

'She has an insidious way of getting what she wants, but it is really Ralph I prefer – I mean, naturally I would be happy to have them both. Are you truly reconsidering?'

'No, but my obstinacy is beginning to bother me a little. That is greater headway than I ever expected you to make. Keep hammering away at me, Miss Harris. Or may I call you Gwendolyn?'

'If you wish.'

'Thank you,' he said, which sounded a formal termination of our visit. He bowed, said good evening, and walked to the door, then walked back to the sitting room and stuck his head in. 'The smoke has cleared. I'll have the chimney cleaned tomorrow.'

'How are your burned fingers?' I asked.

'Badly singed. That will teach me to play with fire.'

'I hoped it would teach you the inefficacy of using two-hundred-year-old articles.'

'I shall *really* leave now, before you remind me of the box stairs. Thank you for a charming evening, Gwendolyn.'

I do not know what charm he could have found in an evening marred with smoking grate, burned fingers, lukewarm tea, and my mother's nervous chatter, but he sounded sincere.

# Chapter Sixteen

*T*he next day is recorded in the family annals as the day Menrod went through the roof. What a time we had next morning, when the man came down from the Manor to clean the chimney. Menrod accompanied him, to see no damage was done to the aged thatch. He brought three mangy brindled cats, which he suggested hopefully Mrs Pudge might like to have, as he could not find Lady, and which I suggested he take home with him when he left. Gwen was in hands with the newly arrived governess, but Ralph, too young for lessons, was along for the sport.

'They will be useful to hunt out the mice in the roof,' he explained.

Mama, Mrs Pudge, her husband, and myself went out to watch the spectacle. The chimney sweep chosen was one of his grooms, a dark youth called Tam. It happened that our ladder did not quite reach the roof, so it was necessary to bring the farm cart out to place the ladder on, with Pudge and Menrod holding the bottom steady. Tam scampered up to the roof, then had his long-handled broom passed up to him. Once atop the roof, he required a box to stand on, for he was not tall enough, nor his arms long enough, to get the broom down the chimney. When the box was passed up, it was too wobbly to stand on, so Menrod had to go up and hold it steady.

'I should have brought another boy with me,' he complained.

'*I* believe it is a man's job. Are you afraid to tackle it, Menrod?' I prodded.

'Certainly not. I happen to be wearing a new jacket that I don't want to get soiled.'

'I will be happy to hold it for you.'

He removed it, folded it carefully, and handed it over to me, glaring angrily the whole time. It was my turn to climb up on the cart and steady the ladder with Pudge, while he went up to the roof, very reluctantly. I believe he was frightened to death of the height, though he was too proud to admit it. He looked timidly over his shoulder as he climbed, and was careful to go in well past the edge once he got up there.

The next thing we knew, there was a terrific bellow from above. I looked in fright, expecting to see Tam tumble from the roof, but I saw nothing for a moment. Soon Tam's head peered over the edge.

'His lordship has fallen through the roof,' he said fearfully.

'Oh, my goodness!' Mama squealed. 'Pudge – Gwendolyn – do something.'

I didn't know whether to be frightened or amused. I went up the ladder with only Pudge steadying it, none too carefully, either. When I saw Menrod's situation, I gave up all thoughts of fright, and tried instead to contain my mirth. He was not in the least danger. One leg had sunk through the thatched roof, up past the knee, but he was not about to fall through the rest of the way. The remainder of his body held him up, very uncomfortably, I should think, with one leg stretched out to distribute the weight, while he more or less sat on the roof.

'Careful, miss,' Tam cautioned. 'That's right where his lordship fell through.'

I picked my way cautiously to him, to try to pull him up. It was futile. The roof was too soft to allow me to stand firm anywhere near him, and he was too heavy. Every time he exerted any pressure himself, he sank deeper. 'How the hell am I going to get out of here?' he demanded.

'You're not. If you don't stop wiggling, you are going to fall through the roof entirely, and break your leg.'

He placed no reliance on my intelligence, but gave a good heave that sent him through nearly to the waist, with still the other leg bent at an awkward position on the thatch. He looked like a giant, one-legged crab.

'Where am I?' he asked.

'On the cottage roof,' I answered, bewildered.

'I know that! What is beneath me, in the cottage?'

'At the southeast side, it must be Mama's room,' I answered.

'Is there a bed to fall on?'

'I'll go below and see. Tap on the ceiling if you can, to let me know exactly where you are. I shall have the bed moved to you.'

'Make it snappy. I'm sinking an inch every second.'

I ran toward the roof's edge. 'Be careful!' he shouted after me.

Mama and Mrs Pudge had overheard our discussion. They went before me up the stairs. It was not necessary for Menrod to tap on the ceiling to give us his exact location. His booted foot had come right through the plaster, to dangle twelve inches into the room. A canopied bed being an impossible thing to move, we three women rushed to bring the truckle cot from a spare room and place it beneath his foot, where he would come landing any moment.

'It's all right. You can drop now,' I called up to him. He could not hear me through the ceiling. Mama ran to the window, opened it, and shouted to him.

There was a great shattering and heaving of the plaster, as he kicked it in, somehow, with his free foot. He landed in a shower of plaster dust, splintered lathes, and chunks of plaster on the truckle bed. When I determined he was not hurt, I said demurely, 'I told you it was impossible to clean the chimney. Thank you for trying.'

'You are welcome, Miss Harris,' he answered, then he lay down, closed his eyes and remained thus, like a corpse, till his panting had subsided. He used what he called his condition of 'shock' to cadge an invitation to remain for lunch. As my prime favorite, Ralph, was with him, his first hints were heeded.

'I feel so shaken up, I had best sit tight a couple of hours,' he pointed out, after Pudge had been pressed into service as a valet to wipe the plaster from his head and clothing.

'If you are to sit like a cushion on our sofa all morning, I wish you would put on your jacket at least,' I requested. 'What would anyone who dropped in think, to see you in shirt sleeves?'

'I doubt Mr Everett would take it amiss,' he replied.

Very little was seen of Ralph on that occasion. Several mice had their homes disturbed by the excitement on the roof, so that Ralph acted as herdsman for the three cats. Menrod had some private words with Tam before sending him back to the Manor – some business or other he was postponing.

Menrod found our sofa, and later my conservatory, so comfortable, there was no budging him. Jocular questions about sending for his valet to bring a change of clothing were answered with another joke.

'Do we dress for dinner? Why not make it a trunk? – I may have to stay for a day or two.'

'You don't match our decor.'

'Paint me yellow – hang a plant on me,' he suggested.

It was very odd the way he stayed so long, but I began to suspect there was a reason for it. He had spoken of his obstinacy in the matter of the children. Mixed in with his foolish chatter, there were a good many pertinent questions designed to discover how life went on at our cottage, day to day. I hoped he was reconsidering his decision to keep them at the Manor. Unfortunately there was no disguising the fact that we led a quiet, sequestered, fairly dull life, one that would not give the children those worldly advantages their uncle considered necessary.

'I hope I am not keeping you from some important engagements, Gwendolyn?' he asked, early on.

'Not in the least. I can give my plants their morning tea while we talk.

He was surprised I did actually water them with diluted tea left over from breakfast. 'They take it straight, I see. No milk or sugar.'

'They are purists. They don't care a fig for coffee, but weak, tepid tea once a week appeals to them.'

'How did you come across this obscure wisdom?'

'I learned it from Sir Harold Milgrove, the Reading botanist.'

'I did not realize you knew him,' Menrod said, brightening at my knowing a learned local gentleman.

'I don't. He does a column in the local newspaper. I should like to meet him. Those two-hundred-year-old rosebushes out front could do with some help. He is an expert on roses. Mama and I toured his rose gardens last season. Delightful.'

'Why do you not call on him, or invite him to call on you?' he asked, astonished I should want to meet him for a decade and never stir a finger to accomplish such a simple aim.

'I don't know him. How should I call on a perfect stranger?'

'It could surely be arranged through a mutual friend. A common interest will always serve as an excuse. Only consider how our mutual guardianship of Ralph and Gwen has brought us together. Last year we were no more than nodding acquaintances; now I feel free to run tame at the cottage. Drop in any time, even through the roof.'

'You can feel free to leave, too, whenever you recover from your shocked condition.'

'You mean that as a facer, I know, but I am flattered. I have a theory . . . that is, when your hostess takes the liberty to hint you away so broadly, you know you are on firm ground. No one would be so farouche as to request a mere acquaintance to leave. That privilege is restricted to good friends. As we are now friends, don't feel it necessary to entertain me. But on the other hand, if you are at liberty, don't take that as a hint to leave, either.'

'I am not likely to leave before I have served all my guests their tea,' I pointed out, lifting the watering pot high to reach a fern that has the place of honor, atop a stone pedestal beside the window. This particular friend, the fern, is troublesome. It is necessary to draw a stool from the corner to reach her. When Menrod saw what I was about, he took the pot from me and watered the plant. This done, he held the pot precariously over my head, and enquired whether I would like a drink while he was about it. I am willing to accept his word that it was an accident four or five drops did indeed fall on me.

'They will do you good,' he assured me, patting the top of my head. 'A green girl needs her tea, as well as a green fern.'

'*Green* girl? I am not seven years old. I passed green four or five years ago.'

'You are hardly withered. I discern a blossom trying to form, after all these years, and wish to give it *every* encouragement.'

'How nice. Does it show promise of being a good, big blossom, or a poor runted thing, like the roses out front?'

'We shan't know till it opens. That must be part of the charm of gardening – waiting to see what shape and color and size a bloom develops.'

'I am interested in the whole plant, not just the flower. I take particular pleasure in finding just the right spot for each – enough sun, but not too much.'

Mrs Pudge came to enquire whether her Lady had yet shown up at the Manor, and heard she had not. She politely declined his offer of one of the brindled cats.

'No, thank you kindly. It wouldn't be the same. I'll just go on looking and waiting. She might come back. It was the mischief and vanity under the tongue of that old black Tom cat that led her off. She'll soon learn her mistake. She'll cry in the daytime, like a sinner.'

'That will be infinitely preferable to her caterwauling at night,' I said after Mrs Pudge had left, her shoulders slumping in grief.

'I could not agree with you more. Those demmed cats have more fun than their owners.'

At lunch hour, our uninvited guest still made no motion of leaving. Not long afterwards, Mr Everett arrived. It was his day for a visit, though it had slipped out of my mind. He was not surprised or dismayed to see Menrod lounging on the sofa with Ralph at his feet, looking at picture books, while Mama and myself danced attendance on them both.

'Good day to you all,' he said, strutting in, knees stiff. 'I see you have had a spot of trouble with your roof, Gwendolyn.'

He heard the story from Menrod, who made much of his fall, complaining of various aches and pains, all with accompanying winces and so on. Everett had a good laugh at our folly. 'What you need is a scaffold,' he told us.

'It is such a big job to build a whole scaffold up the side of the house, only to clean the chimney,' Mama pointed out.

' 'Tis,' he agreed, frowning, 'though there's more than a chimney to do now. There's the roof to be redone as well. There's another route you could go. Broad planks laid atop the thatching would serve your purpose, to distribute the weight, you see. Don't buy them. I've planks aplenty at Oakdene I'll have sent up.'

'Would they not slip off?' I asked, trying to envisage this arrangement.

'What I'll do,' he outlined, taking over the whole project for his own, 'is to have my carpenters bang up a V-shaped contraption to sit over the top of the roof, so it won't fall off. It won't take a minute. I'd do it now, but I am due in an hour at the Dower House.'

I was curious to hear his explanation of this statement. Menrod hid his curiosity no better than I. 'Calling on my step-mother, are you?' he asked.

'Her and Lady Althea. I am taking up my gear for making ices, for the ball. My ice tub, freezing pot, spaddles, cellaret, and so on. Her ladyship has got herself a tin freezing pot, which is why she has such poor luck with her ices. It must be pewter. You can pick up a pewter pot for a sovereign, if you know where to go for it. There is no point stinting on cheap gear; it don't pay off in the long run. The freezing goes on too quickly in the tin pots. The edges are frozen solid before the rest of the stuff is chilled at all. I would be happy to lend them to you as well, Gwendolyn, if you ever find yourself hankering for an ice.'

'Thank you.'

'A four-gallon freezing pot is what I have got,' he continued. I could not think it likely I would ever require four gallons of iced cream, but it was kind of him to offer. 'I have some excellent receipts as well, if you don't know how to stir the stuff up. I thought ices were a new thing in the world, but Lady Althea tells me they have been around forever, since the days of the Medicis.'

'You showed her your gear when she was at Oakdene to see the picture, did you?' Mama asked, with a glint of suspicion in her eyes.

'She's not seen it yet. I offered the loan of it yesterday, when I was at the Dower House,' he answered promptly, with no appearance of guilt. 'I went to have a look at your ice house, Lord Menrod, in case you hadn't enough ice for the iced cream, but I see you are well supplied. My ice house at Oakdene holds twenty-five thousand pounds.'

These statements revealed a closeness between Everett and the ladies that went beyond anything I was aware of. How did he know they planned to serve ices in the first place? He was clearly a pet at the Dower House. I was piqued to learn it, though it was unreasonable of me.

He left in ample time to be at the Dower House before the hour he had spoken of. Mama could not say what she wanted, with Menrod under her nose, but her impatient jiggling in her chair spoke as clearly as words what she thought. Lady Althea was stealing my beau.

Within another sixty minutes I learned Lady Althea held a similar grudge against me. She came dashing down to the cottage to learn why Menrod had spent the entire day thus far with us. She had done no more than accept Everett's ice-making gear from him, learned where Menrod was, and come hounding down after him immediately. Her pretext was to learn how bad his condition was.

'Lady Menrod and I were so worried to hear from Tam you had fallen,' she said earnestly, but there was a stiffness about her lips that spoke of anger. 'Tam said it was not serious, or I would have been here sooner. I thought you had gone on into Reading or elsewhere, when you canceled our luncheon engagement.'

'No, I stayed here, to recover from the shock,' he answered.

'Have you had a doctor?'

'Nothing is broken. I don't want a country sawbones jostling me about,' he replied.

'You would be more comfortable at home in your bed,' was her next inspiration. 'Lady Menrod and I will tend you. Come, now, Menrod, you have battened yourself on Mrs Harris long enough,' she said, but it was *Miss* Harris who received the glaring look.

'You are right, of course,' he agreed, rising from the sofa. He thanked us for our kind attention, then brought another wince of chagrin to Lady Althea's face when he said offhandedly he would be down in the morning to help Mr Everett tend to the roof and the chimney.

'Let Everett do it,' Lady Althea said at once. 'You will only fall and hurt yourself again.'

'I shall let his men do it, but it is my cottage, and I want it done properly, to retain its historical flavor. I shall go into Reading now and arrange to have a thatcher here.'

'No, you must come home and recuperate,' she insisted.

'I am feeling much better since your arrival, Althea,' he answered ambiguously. She took it as a compliment, but it seemed to me he was anxious to escape her ministrations.

'You promised you would help us with the ball tomorrow,' she said. 'It is practically upon us, and there are a dozen things to be done. The seating arrangement for dinner, for instance. . . .' she began, then stopped quickly. Menrod cast an embarrassed look at us, for of course Mama and I were not invited to the preparty dinner.

'That has nothing to do with me – I left it in your hands completely. Menu, wines, guests. . . .' he said pointedly, to exculpate himself in our eyes, though neither of us expected to be invited for dinner. That was for particularly close friends and relatives, mostly coming from some distance and remaining overnight.

They left very soon afterwards, Ralph going with his uncle into Reading, while Althea drove back to the Dower House, her face pink with vexation.

'There is the boldest hussy in England,' Mama declared,

exhaling angry puffs of frustration. 'Having no luck with Mr Everett, she is throwing her cap at Lord Menrod, feathers and all.'

'You have got it backwards, Mama. Having so little luck with Menrod, she is making a pitch for Everett, to incite her first choice to jealousy. She would never *marry* Mr Everett. She is an earl's daughter. She'll look higher than a lumber dealer for a match.'

'That explains why Menrod has stuck to us like a burr all day, preventing us from getting a thing done. He used us as an excuse to escape her luncheon party. That is why he hung around so long. I could not make heads or tails of it, for there was not a *thing* to do to amuse him, but it is all clear now. Next time he wants to get away from her, I hope he goes somewhere else. You notice Lady Althea did not include us in her dinner party. She withheld those invitations on purpose, Gwendolyn, because she fears you are dangling after Menrod, the ninny-hammer. As though he would *ever* have an interest in you! I remember to this day how he carried on when Peter offered for Hettie, and *he* was only the younger son.'

'What *did* he say, exactly?'

'Every unpleasant thing you can think of. I cannot remember the words exactly, except for a few phrases, but he felt the match very much beneath Lord Peter. It is what comes of his passing a summer in the country, with no *decent* company or occupations,' he said, as though we were not *decent*. I will not soon forgive him for that.'

'He did not mean indecent, only provincial – lacking in cultural refinement. He places great store in such frivolity.'

Mrs Pudge had sauntered in, her hands hidden beneath her white apron, to give her the appearance of an expectant mother. She listened to the speeches, then set her head aslant to condemn the whole house of Menrod.

'Our Hettie was a deal too decent for Lord Peter. Only see where it got her, perished in the sea. Folks that call their lands after their own names, in their pride, all perish like the beasts, and so do the foolish girls that make the mistake of marrying them. Men of high degree are all a lie, including Menrod. I know Lady is at his barn, with that devil cat. Why else would *he* disappear from the yard the same time as her? I'll send Pudge up to have a look about for her. Trying to palm me off with that mangy old brindled cat a dozen years old. He wanted to get rid of it so he wouldn't have to feed her. She's a good mice-catcher, though, to give the devil her due.'

This led to the thought that my mother's room no longer had a full ceiling, but a great gaping hole, which would allow the mice to enter. The remainder of our day was spent tucking old papers and blankets in to seal up the gap, cleaning up the plaster, airing another room for Mama for the night, and later, chasing the half dozen or so mice that had taken advantage of the hole to get into the house.

It was difficult to sleep, with the strong possibility one shared her room with a mouse or two. I left two tall candles burning all night. There was plenty of time to think of everything, including Menrod's speech regarding passing a season in the country, with no decent company. His notion of decent, in a bride, would include a good education, the knowledge of French, pianoforte, an appreciation of the arts, and of course a large dowry. A few titles and honors decking the family tree would not go amiss. He was not likely to find any such paragon hereabouts except Lady Althea, and he was so eager to escape her that he had chosen instead to go sequester himself in a small cottage till she had run him to ground. He had not appeared bored with his day, either. It had even occurred to me once or twice – when he was watering my head, for instance, that he might be falling into Lord Peter's trap. His manner, at any rate, had traveled to the very perimeter of a friend's, and was beginning to go beyond it. As he was so very much aware of the dangers lurking in the countryside, I felt sure he would leave soon. Yes, as soon as the six weeks' interim custody were up, he would go away.

# Chapter Seventeen

*a*fter my poor sleep, I was awakened by a loud hammering outside my window at eight o'clock in the morning. Still groggy, I raised the window to see Mr Everett ordering his three carpenters about. He had a piece of paper in his hand, on which he had doubtlessly drawn a careful sketch of the planking to go on the roof. I made a hasty toilette, had a cup of tea and a piece of toast, and went outdoors to greet him.

'I have decided to give your roof a new subfloor,' he told me merrily. Looking around to the back of the house, I saw a huge load of lumber stood ready for the job. 'We'll just have the old moldy thatch yanked off, and nail down some fresh lumber beneath. It will not interfere with the ancient looks of the place, which is what his lordship is concerned with.'

'Menrod is coming down later. You had better await his arrival before removing the thatch, Mr Everett.'

'We discussed it at my place last night. He is in agreement.'

'You're sure? You thought he would have no objection to the brass railing either, but he was very upset,' I reminded him.

'We actually talked about it. He took his mutton with me last night, he and the quiet little lad, Ralph. They were in Reading to see the thatcher, and stopped off at Oakdene. I put it to him you ladies do a deal of complaining about the dampness of the thatch and the mice, and he feels a good new wooden roof beneath the thatch will keep you drier.'

The season in the country was indeed working a peculiar spell on Menrod, if he chose to spend an evening with a lumber merchant. I was quite simply amazed to hear it.

If I ever have the misfortune again to be living in a house whose roof is being replaced, I shall remove to an inn for the duration. It was such an interesting show that every rattle in the neighborhood with nothing better to do came and stood, gawking. It was a strong inducement to go indoors and draw the curtains, but within, there was the awful pounding and hammering overhead, echoing like the inside of a drum, shaking the whole house. Menrod came riding down at ten o'clock to join the throng.

'How lively for you.' He smiled. 'A full-fledged circus going forth in your yard. You should set up a gingerbread stall, and make some profit from it.'

'If I had known what was involved, I would have opted for the mold and the mice and the smoking grate. My head is throbbing from the din. I suppose it will go on all day.'

'It won't be done in a day,' he pointed out reasonably. 'The floor will be done in two or three, however, and once the thatchers get to work, the banging will be finished. They work quietly.'

Mr Everett walked over to greet Menrod. 'The lads will be done in jig time. You'll notice the fine cured lumber I have supplied you. Well dried – I would not be ashamed to have it in my own house. Quite an entertainment for the kiddies,' he said, including several octogenarians in the word.

'A terrible racket to saddle the ladies with,' Menrod mentioned.

'It is. We are a pair of fools not to have thought to invite them to put up with one or the other of us while it goes on. You and your mama run down to Oakdene, Gwendolyn. You will be perfectly comfortable there.'

'I was just inviting Gwendolyn and her mother to spend the day at the Manor,' Menrod said when he read the dismay on my face. If he was astute, he saw no diminution of it at his own offer. I hardly knew which house was less desirable to go to. Accepting Everett's kind offer would look like encouragement of his suit, while going to the Manor so close to the time of the ball would put us under Lady Althea's feet. We would be about as welcome as poison ivy to her. Home was suddenly seen to be not at all so bad as before.

I took the coward's way out. 'Mama spoke of going into town for a few hours,' I lied.

'That settles it, then,' Everett jumped in quickly. 'You will stop off at Oakdene on your way home, and stay there while the work goes forth. I'll halt the lads a bit early, to let you dine in peace. Unless you would care to sup with me. . . .'

With the omission of dining at Oakdene, we followed Everett's plan. We took lunch in Reading, spent an afternoon at Oakdene, gazing at all its finery, like tourists at a museum. We were taken to the attics to see the cherry wainscotting, which was very handsome. The slightest hint of curiosity saw the rug removed from one of the studies, to show us the parquetry unicorn laid into the pattern, also very handsome. We returned at four, at which time Everett called the work to a stop. Kind schemer that he is, he had worked only half the roof at a time, so that one side was all done, and the thatch not yet disturbed on the other side.

'We'll give the lads tomorrow off, so that you and your mama may be home in peace to ready yourselves for the party. I hope my people took care of you at Oakdene?'

'Superb care, thank you so very much.'

'After the ball, you will come to spend a few days, if you like, while this little job is finished up for you.'

We should have asked him to dinner, but with both of us away all afternoon, it had not been arranged, so was impossible. We ate a simple omelette ourselves, in the deafening silence that followed the day's hammering.

The next day was blissfully peaceful. We saw neither Everett nor Menrod, the children, nor anyone else. Though quiet, it was not dull, with a ball to prepare for. No peacock, I had not had a new gown made, but I did hang my best blue crepe on the line to air in the morning. During the afternoon, while I was working to revive my complexion with some lemon juice and oatmeal, I toyed with my hair, wondering what the deuce a *victime* do might be.

Mama thought it was a style popular during the French Revolution, favored by Victims there and aped in England by society. If so, it cannot have been the highest kick of fashion. The Revolution was twenty-five years old. She pointed out to me in a two-year-old fashion magazine a style that was similar to the *victime*. I tried puffing my curls around my head but looked a perfect quiz, so abandoned the idea. Pearls were my jewelry, a single strand of good-sized pearls given to me by my father's mother. With my new white kid gloves, I felt elegant in the extreme. Mama too had her navy silk aired, and wore her pearls, larger and longer than my own. She wore a white shawl with a long fringe, to cover her bare arms.

We were no sooner announced and made welcome by the hostess, the guest of honor, and Lord Menrod, ranged in state at the stair landing, than Mr Everett came trotting up to us. It scarcely left us time to assess Lady Althea's toilette – a beautiful bronze taffeta, very much the shade of hair, and a set of emeralds much darker than her eyes, and much more beautiful.

'A dandy do,' Everett said, rubbing his hands. 'I was surprised not to see you sit down at dinner. Lady Althea said they had so many houseguests it was impossible, but it seems to me they could have squeezed in a couple of extra chairs. Menrod was put out about it, and so was I. I would not have come, had I known you were omitted.'

'We are not on such close terms with Lady Althea as you are coming to be,' Mama told him.

'How was the dinner?' I enquired.

'A fair meal,' he said judiciously. 'I expected to see some better seafood than prawns and oysters, but the roast was tasty. My own cook does the fowl better, I think. A fine bit of carving there, around the oval mirrors,' he said on the next breath. We strolled toward the mirrors to admire this specimen of wood, that was bound to interest Mr Everett.

There was plenty of wood to catch his attention. He traced a wooden bunch of grapes with his finger, to determine whether it had been sanded after carving or the artist had worked his knife so skilfully as to leave no rough edges. 'The grain of it looks like oak,' he said doubtfully. 'Oak is a hard wood for ornamental carving.'

Menrod and Lady Althea opened the minuet. My first partner was Mr Everett. Mama sat with the matrons for half an hour to observe the ladies' toilettes. She would soon remove to the card parlor. I went to speak to her and her friends before they left. There was a flurry of gossip going forth.

'Mrs Tighe thinks a match is in the offing between Lady Althea and Menrod,' she communicated to me, on a high whisper. 'Their opening the ball together looks very much like it.'

It looked like simple protocol to me, as she was the guest of honor, but some ladies who had attended the dinner were whispering otherwise. They were closer friends than ourselves to the lady concerned, so some credence had to be placed on their word. Mr Everett listened, frowning in disbelief.

'It is not what Lady Althea intimated to me,' he said. 'Just friends, she described the relationship. Friends and connections,

I believe she said.'

I stood up with Mr Farrell, the local M.P., next; then, at the end of that dance, Menrod appeared at my elbow. 'There is a young gentleman who is eager to see you, Gwendolyn,' he told me.

I excused myself from Farrell and followed Menrod from the floor, pleasantly curious to learn what gentleman desired my acquaintance. Seeing no one waiting, I said, 'Where is he hiding, in the attic?' for he was heading to the staircase.

'No, his bedroom. Ralph wants to see you decked out in ballroom style. Very nice, too,' he complimented dutifully, his gaze including my hairstyle.

'There's a setdown for me! I thought I had attracted a new beau.'

'Disenchanted with the old ones so soon?'

'You are too kind to grant me more than one. Mr Everett is my sole conquest to date.'

'Don't be so modest. I have had my ears scorched the past twenty-four hours for chasing after an engaged lady. By my stepmother,' he added.

'She is imaginative, to find a romance in your falling through the roof.'

'Reality is no bar to a lady's imagination. She has imagined me to be on the verge of an offer to her cousin for the past few weeks, despite my care to avoid the lady. Unhandsome of me to broach such a subject, but I know your discretion is to be counted on. If you should chance to overhear any rumors of my imminent engagement, you may feel yourself free to squelch them.'

'We had already figured out why your condition of shock lasted so many hours,' I told him, with a knowing look.

'Having exerted your poor little wits to such a wrong end, you will now put them to better use, if you please. I refer to our niece. The wretch talked Althea into allowing her to come down after dinner to make a curtsy to the guests, and is now at work on me to let her attend the ball.'

'At six years of age! That is precocious of her!'

'Exactly what I think. She insists she was allowed to do so in India, when she was only five.'

'Hettie would never be so foolish. She's bamming you.'

'I told her I would ask your opinion.'

'Kind of you to cast *me* in the role of ogre.'

We went to the nursery, where the children sat with a servant, decked out in their best togs. Gwen ran to me to throw her arms around me. 'I *knew* you would come, Aunt!' she beamed. 'Tell Uncle I can go down to the ball, just for a moment. I only want to see everyone all dressed up so fine. Ralph wants to go too, don't you, Ralph?' she asked.

'Yes,' Ralph said simply, his eyes as big as sovereigns.

'It is close to nine o'clock. These children should have been in bed an hour ago,' I told Menrod. I was cross at his stunt of drawing me into his problem. 'You know it is impossible, children. You are much too young to attend a ball.'

'Lady Althea said it would be all right,' Gwen tried next. 'And Mama *always* let us take one peek.'

'It is too late now. If you were to have had one peek, it should have been at the beginning.'

'You're *mean!*' Gwen charged, a tear forming in her eyes, while her lower lip trembled. 'We waited all this time. If Mama and Papa were alive, we would be allowed to go. You don't love us. You *hate* us!' Her tears and tantrum swelled in unison, till at last Ralph joined in the sobbing from sheer nervousness. I wanted to box her ears.

'This will do you no good, Gwen,' I said severely. Menrod accepted my dictum, but did not support me verbally, so Gwen turned to him.

'Please, Uncle,' she sobbed, her shoulders racking with emotion.

'It is too late. Go to bed now.'

'But Aunt Althea is going to bring us an ice. She promised she would. I want an ice!'

'The ices are not ready yet.'

Her bawling became louder, so loud I feared she would be heard belowstairs. 'That is enough of that, Gwen,' I said firmly. 'Put them to bed,' I added, to the servant.

'I *won't* go to bed,' she insisted, stomping her stubborn feet on the floor. When the servant girl reached for her, Gwen flailed out with her hands, giving her such a scratch she drew blood. I had seen enough of ill manners. I pulled Gwen off and gave her a shaking. 'You will apologize at once, Gwen, and you will then go to bed.'

'I don't have to do what *you* say. *You're* not my guardian. I don't want to live with you. I hate you.'

'*I* am your guardian,' Menrod said, taking a swift stride toward her and grabbing her arms, 'and I say you will apologize to Miss Acres before going to your bed. If there is another word from you, you will remain in your room for twenty-four hours.'

'*You're* not my guardian either!' she shouted back. 'Neither of you can be my guardian. I want my Aunt Althea.'

Menrod dragged her from the room by one arm, took her out the hallway, shoved her into her own room, and locked the door, then apologized to Miss Acres on her behalf. 'Keep an ear to the door, but don't go in to her,' he told the servant. 'Let her put herself to bed. She'll soon be worn out with this performance. She must learn she doesn't profit by this sort of carry-on. You run along to bed too, Ralph.'

'I'm sorry, Uncle,' he said humbly.

'It's not your fault. A boy would not behave so foolishly. Good night.' As he went down the hall, screams and shouts came echoing through Gwen's door. I was upset at the unpleasant interlude and did not want to go back to the ball at once.

'We'll collect our nerves with a drink,' Menrod suggested.

'A glass of wine would not go amiss,' I agreed.

'A glass of wine? You are easily calmed. I intend gulping a quart of brandy. Let us have it brought up. If we go downstairs, we'll be overtaken by unwanted company. Come in here – it is my late mother's sitting room,' he said, opening a door farther down the hallway. A servant encountered along the way was sent for wine and glasses.

Menrod was as upset as I was at the affair. He sat on the corner of a small sofa, clenching and unclenching his fingers, hardly aware of my presence. He wore a distracted expression. I did not urge any conversation with him; I was busy thinking myself. My major thought was that taking complete charge of Gwen was a thing beyond me. She was very spoilt, a manipulator, turning to one of us when the other did not follow her wishes, and in the end turning to Aunt Althea when we both held out against her.

'That wench has got badly out of hand,' he said a moment later. I agreed enthusiastically. 'You handled her well,' he complimented. 'I have been too soft with her, pitying her because of her orphaned state. She is quick enough to have sensed it, to take advantage.'

'She is not even truthful. Hettie would not have let her attend balls in India. She wrote me of the customs there, and never mentioned that one.'

'I know full well Peter would not have permitted it. Her orphaned state is always called to our attention when she is thwarted. I should not have dragged you into it.'

'Why did you? Was it to show me how impossible the task is that I have been wanting to undertake? If that was your aim, you have succeeded marvelously. I don't believe I could handle Gwen, with Mama and Mrs Pudge always there to cater to her every whim. She is a great favorite at home.'

'I am not so underhanded as that!' he exclaimed offended. 'I wondered if I was being too severe, that's all. You too are involved in their upbringing. It was of some concern to you, as well as myself.'

'How could you possibly have considered taking them down to a ball?'

'Lady Althea thought it permissible. Whatever else she may know or not know, she is well versed in social etiquette. I do not attend many country balls. Customs change – I thought perhaps it was some recent innovation.'

'I haven't heard of it, but if it were to be done, it should have been done for the opening minuet.'

'I could hardly discuss it when I was on duty welcoming guests. One likes to pull crows in comparative private.'

'It is a pity, but let us not permit it to spoil the whole evening.'

'We must sail a tighter ship in future, Gwendolyn. When *I* refused her the new riding habit, she weaseled it out of you. When *you* refused the mink tippet to go with it, she got the fur-lined cape out of me. I have a good mind to renege on that promise. And when all else fails, she trots to Lady Menrod or Althea. They are as bad as your mother and Mrs Pudge – putty in her hands.'

'Thank God Ralph at least is biddable. I daresay he too will become more difficult as he grows older. You were correct to deny me the privilege of raising them. I won't fight the custody application you have made.'

'Do! Please! I am fed up to the eyeballs with Gwen. I was within ames-ace of giving her a good thrashing. Earlier today, when I refused to let her wear my mother's diamonds, she threatened to run away to you, who are always so kind and sweet to her.'

'It's really Ralph I like.'

'You like him too much. The girl needs a firm hand – like yours,' he said, taking my fingers in his.

'No, no – I would never be able to spank her as I ought. I hesitate to lob an inch off my plants, Menrod. To spank a child would be beyond me. You keep her.'

'She'll get dreadfully spoiled when I am away, bear-leading all the servants,' he pointed out, half joking now.

'The cottage is too small. You said so yourself.'

'Peter had money. I'll turn it over to you – Mrs Livingstone's house is empty.'

'Don't grovel. It doesn't become you.'

'We'll work something out.'

I extracted my fingers from his, without much opposition. 'It was a bad idea I had. It seemed like Fate, at first, as if God had meant me to have the children, as I had none of my own, and nothing else that mattered very much in my life.'

'We men are conceited enough to think women were put on earth to nurture us, and we them. You were putting the cart before the horse. It was a husband you should have been seeking, not the children.'

'Well, I am no longer seeking the children, at least. I would not have Gwen in my charge for all the cream in Devon.'

'You refuse to share the burden with me, then?'

'I don't mean to say I am abandoning them entirely. I will always be at the cottage, to give a hand in any way I can.'

'That was not what I had in mind.'

'I know it. Pray forget what you had in mind. You had your chance to be rid of her, and unwisely lost it.'

There was a tap at the open door. Glancing to it, I saw Lady Althea entering, with an angry, fixed smile on her face.

'What is this awful tale Gwen tells me, about your not letting her down to see the ball, Miss Harris?' she enquired.

'You appear to have heard the story,' I answered.

'Oh, heartless! How *can* you be so unfeeling? She is sobbing and weeping. Let us take her down, just for a moment,

Menrod. I promised her some of the iced cream before she went to bed, and it will not be ready till midnight. Mr Everett – your friend, Miss Harris – says it should be readied at the very last moment. Gwen is under your care, Menrod. What do you say?' she asked, with a coaxing smile.

He had arisen upon her entry. She did not take a seat either, which left me looking up at them from my chair, too weary to arise. 'We have agreed she is much too young to attend a ball,' Menrod told her.

'*Agreed?* Miss Harris has dictated, you mean. Previous to her arrival, it was agreed Gwen and Ralph would be allowed down for a few minutes.'

'It was discussed, not agreed. Our decision has been taken,' he replied firmly.

Her eyes narrowed for a fraction of a second, then grew wider in vexation. Her nostrils also flared. From my seat below, she looked closer to ugly than I had ever seen her look. She sniffed, throwing back her copper head. 'I find it odd Miss Harris should intrude into our affairs,' she said.

'The affair is her business and mine – no one else's.'

'This is a change of face! You have complained often enough about her interference. . . .' She stopped in mid-speech, to stare mutely at Menrod. I looked to see what in his reaction had brought her to a halt at this interesting juncture. His jaws were clenched in anger. He looked ready to strike her.

'Well, I see I am interrupting your tête-à-tête. So odd you choose to abandon your own ball. You *will* be down later, when Miss Harris releases you?' she asked.

'When we have finished our *private* discussion,' he agreed.

She glared once at us both, turned sharply, and left, without another word.

'You are released, Menrod. Our private discussion is about over,' I said.

He shook his head and laughed. 'She's an impossible woman,' he said, dismissing her. I found the incident anything but laughable. I was boiling mad, as much at his having complained of my interference as anything else. He calmly poured two more glasses of wine, raised his glass, and made a toast.

'To your continued interference,' he said, with a bold smile.

'I'll drink to that. And to your kindness in relating it to Lady Althea.'

We drank ceremoniously. '*Initially* I may have made a few comments. . . . That stiff jaw does not encourage me to continue,' he pointed out.

'Good. I have had enough of this subject. Shall we go back down now?'

'By all means. I think people ought to have a dance or two, when they attend a ball. You have not stood up with me yet,' he said, offering his hand to aid me up from my seat.

We went together, arm in arm, down the lovely curving staircase, without talking. My mood softened to pleasure, to see the chandeliers sparkling, the beautifully gowned ladies and black-coated gentlemen walking to and fro, standing in clusters all around the hallway and on into the ballroom. There was a pause in the music, which sent many couples off to the refreshment parlor.

Lady Althea was there, complaining to Lady Menrod, who looked uncomfortable to be in the middle of a quarrel. She gave us a worried, placating smile. Menrod, to spite them, took a closer grip on my arm and inclined his head to smile at me in a besotted way.

'I do believe your friend Everett is measuring my hallway up for refurbishing,' he said, indicating a corner, where my friend was indeed scrutinizing an intricate piece of carving to discover the secret of its smoothness.

When Everett glanced up and saw us, Menrod bolted in unseemly haste toward the ballroom, to lose himself and me in the throng. Lines were beginning to form for a country dance. 'I am not up to such a scramble, after the past half hour's annoyance,' he declared, echoing my own feelings. 'I'll ask the musicians to play some waltzes.'

'If you want to empty the floor and dance solo, go ahead. Hardly anyone waltzes yet, here in the country.'

'Do *you* waltz?' he asked.

'Yes, badly.'

'If even *you* have attempted it, I am convinced my other guests will be adept by now.'

After that vote of confidence, I was careful to stay off his feet. Our conversation was on the most mundane of topics. He mentioned the troublesome necessity of having to plaster Mama's ceiling, enquired whether Lady had turned up and heard she had not, made a few bad jokes about Oakdene and my mistress-ship of it. He only put on his doting smile when Lady Althea came into view. On those few occasions, his frosty eyes melted as he stared at me in a bewitched way.

'Do you really think you are fooling anyone with this lovesick performance?' I asked him.

'What *can* you mean?' he asked, feigning puzzlement.

'I mean those rumors that we are to hear an engagement. You are *using* me to show the world you don't intend to marry Lady Althea.'

'Who else should I use? But really it is only Althea and Lady Menrod I have to show. What do *you* care? You're safe – engaged to Mr Everett. What *is* the status of that peculiar engagement, at the moment?'

'You know I am not engaged to him.'

'He is more generous in allowing himself to be used than you are.'

'You don't have to remind me. He is criminally good-natured. He makes me feel guilty, he is so generous.'

'You'll feel much better when you learn the reason for his eagerness to wed you.'

'Did he tell you?' I asked.

'He was kind enough to give me his reason, when I asked,' he admitted, holding in his laughter.

'Why did you ask? It's none of your business.'

'Simple curiosity, madam. Life is dull in the country, with no petty intrigues going forward. I might have been worse employed.'

I realized the significance of that speech, but was too curious to dwell on it. 'What did he say? What was his reason?'

'I have a theory regarding bad news. Hardly an original one – it comes to us from the Greeks. I never transmit bad news if I can help it. It redounds to the discredit of the transmitter. Why should *I* receive the poke in the eye that is due Mr Everett?'

'That bad? This is a mystery. He knows I have no money. He can see for himself what I look like. What is it? Tell me, Menrod. I promise I won't hit you.'

'Ladies' promises are writ on water. Usually hot water.'

'It's not . . . he is not *sorry* for me? Is it pity – is that it?' I demanded, mortified to suspect I had discovered the humiliating truth. His generosity might well take this form.

'No, no – hardly that bad. Or on the other hand, you might consider it worse. I would be the one to pity you, if you accepted him. He goes in for such an abundance of things. A *dozen* of them – really!'

'Is he setting up a harem?'

'No, not a harem. Who is to say he wouldn't go on to try for a baker's dozen too? There would be no end to it.'

My curiosity soared higher, and to make it worse, the dance

was ending. 'You must tell me. You can't leave me like this,' I said urgently.

'I often say that to the ladies. It don't do a bit of good, Gwendolyn. Don't ask again. It's not nice to throw a tantrum at a ball.'

The music ended, confronting us with that embarrassing moment when a lady is in a gentleman's arms, and more aware of it than when the music is playing. He looked down into my eyes, with one of his satirical smiles forming. 'If you feel you *must* know, ask Ev. He'll tell you without blinking. He's told everyone else in town.'

'I hate you.' I smiled sweetly, the smile for Althea's benefit. I disengaged myself from his arms, as he seemed to have forgotten it was time for it.

'I knew how it would be! I have a theory about violent emotions, however.'

'You had better remove yourself from my sight, before that old Grecian theory about the bearer of bad news is fulfilled.'

'You haven't heard the bad news yet.'

'I know it is bad, or you wouldn't be smiling. I have a theory of my own as well.'

'I *adore* theories,' he said, tucking my arm under his to leave the floor. 'Please let me hear it.'

'You are making this whole story up to annoy me. Liars ought to be beaten.'

'Severely,' he agreed amiably. 'That is a demmed sparse theory, by the by. It wants refining. Are you interested to hear mine, regarding violent emotions?'

'No.'

'Liars ought to be beaten,' he reminded me. 'Instead, I shall hit you over the head with my stunning theory, which I developed with only a little help from Lord Byron. It is really quite intriguing. Emotions are reversible, like quilts. The other side of hate is love, and vice versa. It is the absence of emotion that is dangerous. Once you manage to get a lady into a pelter, she is as good as won. Tell me truthfully now, do you *hate* Everett?'

'Not yet. I haven't heard why he wants to marry me.'

'You don't love him, either, and you never will.'

'I never said I did, or would.'

'True, but you said you *hate* me,' he pointed out, raising one finger to wag at me.

My violent emotion felt not the slightest urge to reverse itself. 'I think I am beginning to hate you too,' he added, with a curiously warm smile, just before he turned aside to ask another lady to dance.

# Chapter Eighteen

I could only conclude Menrod had drunk more wine than was good for him. I expected to see him topple over dead drunk before the night was through. Actually I saw little more of him, except his head and shoulders through the throng of dancers. He was being flirtatious with every eligible lady at the ball, except Lady Althea. To show his disdain for her, he did not stand up with her again the whole night. He was the host, and nothing more, where she was concerned.

Mr Everett was more solicitous of my welfare. He came strutting back for another dance after dinner. 'How did you like the ices?' he enquired, as they were his contribution to the party.

'Very nice.'

'It was the pewter pots that turned the trick for the ladies,' he told me. 'There is no making a decent unslivered ice with a tin freezing pot. Shall we stand up and have another jig? I like a country tune. I begin to think I must have a ball at Oakdene. Lady Althea says she would give us a hand with arranging it.'

'I doubt she will linger long in the neighborhood after this ball,' I told him.

'She has indicated she will stick around for a while,' he answered.

'Has she indeed?' I asked, always surprised at his intimacy with her. 'I begin to think she is setting her tiara for you, Mr

Everett,' I said, to roast him.

A girlish blush suffused his face. 'Heh heh – I would be aiming high, to go for an earl's daughter. But it is only a thought, after all. In the eyes of the world, I am engaged to *you* at the present, and very happy I'd be if you said yes, too.'

It was my chance to discover what he had told Menrod, and I was not about to miss it. 'Let us skip the country dance,' I said. 'Shall we go to the refreshment parlor instead?'

'There won't be a soul there, immediately after dinner,' he pointed out.

'Precisely.'

I walked quickly toward it, with Everett stiff-kneeing it beside me. Menrod was at the ballroom door. He raised his brows and gave me an arch smile. 'The moment of truth,' he said softly as I strode past, ignoring him.

'A dandy party,' Everett complimented.

The parlor was as private as I could wish. 'Dare I hope you have brought me here to give your consent to wear my ring at last, Gwendolyn?' Everett asked.

'Mr Everett, why do you want to marry me?' I asked baldly.

He nodded his approval, or at least consent, to the question. He thought a moment, then spoke. 'I can see what may have set you wondering about it, as you are not so young or so pretty as you once were,' he began, not maliciously, but as a reasonable man answering a reasonable question. I stood mute with astonishment, while an incipient fury gathered in my bosom.

'Please continue,' I invited.

'I was about to. The reasons are pretty clear, I think. A man of my age and in my position ought to have a wife. I have a large fortune to leave someone, and would prefer to leave it to my own flesh and blood. My brother Thomas has a daughter, but she would only run through my hard-earned cash. I would prefer to leave it to an Everett, a chip off this very old block, you might say. So first off, you are genteel – you speak well, have good connections due to your sister's marriage, have a good reputation, seem to manage the cottage well enough, and all that. Second off, and really the most important thing in my eyes, you will make a good mother. I plan a large nursery – eight or nine lads, throw in a few daughters to please yourself, and you are looking at a dozen kiddies.'

'Why not a baker's dozen?' I asked stiffly.

'The more the merrier. I know you are fond of kiddies; you even find a tender spot for your little backward nevvie. To top it all off, I *like* you. You are a good, sensible gel, ladylike, without putting on fine airs. I don't have to point out the advantages of the match to yourself. You know what I have to offer. I'm willing to take your mama along into the bargain, and even your sister's kiddies if the case goes in your favor, which Menrod assures me it won't. As well hang for a sheep as a lamb. There's room for them all. An even fifty bedchambers await you at Oakdene. Wait, I tell a lie. I knocked a wall down between a pair of them, leaving us forty-nine, but one of them is a whopper.'

'Forty-nine should be sufficient.'

'So is it a bargain, my girl?' he asked heartily.

'I am very sensible of the honor you do me, Mr Everett, but I really must decline.'

'I have left out the best part, the settlement. I am willing to settle a substantial sum on you. What do you have to say to twenty-five thousand in your own right, eh?'

'Very generous, but I still must decline.'

'It is true what they're whispering, then. You are dangling after the title. You'll catch cold at that. Lady Althea tells me there is no possibility of your nabbing Menrod. He cavorts with duchesses and princesses in the city, and has no opinion at all of country-bred girls. He would never settle for a minister's dowerless daughter. You'll not do better than George Everett,' he told me, prodding his chest with his index finger a couple of times, to make clear he spoke of himself.

'I could do much worse, but my mind is made up.'

'Then we'd best put the notice into the papers that it is over – or a mistake. Word it up any way you choose, but do it right away, if you will be so kind.'

'You may depend on it, it will be in tomorrow's paper.'

'Not unless you take the notice to Reading tonight. Let us look for it the day after tomorrow.'

'It will be done tonight,' I answered firmly. 'It is up to you. So I am free, then?'

'Perfectly free.'

'It is an odd world, surely,' he said, pulling out his white box to admire the ring. 'I had a notion the ball might put you into a marrying mood, and brought this along with me. She's a dandy ring. It set me back. . . .'

'You will find someone to appreciate it,' I told him. My anger dissolved. I felt sorry for him, with all his worldly goods, and no one on whom to bestow them.

'We'll remain good friends. I don't want to be at odds with my neighbors. It is not as if we had ever been lovers, but only friends, and we won't let this stand in the way of our relations. I'll finish up the roof, just as though we were to be married. Though I suppose there will be no harm in letting Menrod bear the expense now, as he wants to do.'

'By all means, let him.'

'We'll be back tomorrow to do it, now that the ball is over. I think I shall have brandied ices at my ball,' he said. That quickly he put aside the memory of our recent talk.

'That will be lovely.'

'Lady Althea has a receipt for it. If we are finished our talk, I'll go along and pester her for it now. Unless you want to join in the tail end of the dance?' he asked punctiliously.

'I will just stay here and rest for a moment.'

'I'll get you a glass of wine. Afraid I cannot offer champagne. . . .' He insisted when I refused.

I sat with an unwanted glass of wine between my fingers, reviewing my disgrace, and my anger with Everett. A female servant came to refresh the ice tray in which the punch sat. She smiled; I smiled back, neither of us speaking. Another form appeared at the door. From the corner of my eye, I noticed the black jacket, and realized it was a guest, to whom I would be required to make some polite speech.

'Is it safe to come in?' Menrod called from the doorway.

'Enter at your own peril.'

He advanced at a tentative pace. 'That heaving bosom tells me you have asked Everett the question, and worse, that he has answered, with his usual disarming candor.'

'That man is an outrage!'

'He hasn't much breeding, I fear, but he plans to do a deal of it. I admire his choice of mate.'

'I am not a brood mare.'

'Think of yourself as a plant, sending out tender shoots. You will make an excellent mama. It would be good for you too, Gwendolyn, to have children to water and nurse, instead of plants.'

'I prefer plants.'

'They're friendly,' he agreed, taking a chair beside me. 'A trifle lacking in conversation. . . .'

'They are not lacking in manners and consideration, at least.'

'I have a well-behaved fern in my study you might like to meet. He tells me he is thinking of getting married. His spores are all in an uproar – it is the season that accounts for it.'

'I have had enough for one night. And the wretch even called Ralph "backward" again. I should have hit him.'

'I was sure you would. I loitered outside the door in case I should have to bolt to his aid.'

'I am going home now. Thank you for the interesting evening, Menrod.'

'*Mi casa, su casa*, as they say in Spain. They have such charming manners there, between brawls. Did you – ah – get the situation straightened out with Everett?'

'Perfectly straight.'

'The next step is to inform the *beau monde*, or the few *beaux ardents* that will be interested, at least.'

'This conversation would be more intelligible to *me* if we both spoke English.'

'I speak in foreign tongues when I am upset – excited.'

'I don't see what *you* have to be upset about!'

'I too am interested in the outcome. Coyness and vacillation are all well and good in a maiden, but there comes a time, you know, when we fellows like to know where we stand, and like others to know it too.'

'You can read the retraction in tomorrow's paper, if you are interested.'

'I *am* interested, but I shan't be reading it. I owe myself a holiday, after this sojourn in the country. There is nothing so debilitating as a long rest.'

'Are you going to London?'

'No, the Season is not on yet. I am going to Brighton.'

'Oh.' I digested this for a moment, then discovered a troublesome point. 'You're running away from Gwen's wrath!' I charged. 'You are trying to *stick* me with the task of calming her down, placating her, while you jaunt about the seaside with Prinny and his rackety friends.'

'You wrong me; every way you wrong me, Gwendolyn,' he answered, shaking his head sadly. 'I am not such a paltry fellow as to flee the wrath of a child. I am taking it with me – both the wrath and the child. It is the full-grown woman's wrath I am fleeing.'

'I would not reward her for her tantrum.'

'Was there ever such a *dissatisfied* woman as you! You complain that I leave her, then that I take her with me. What would you have me do? Stay? Say the word, and it will be done.'

'I don't want you to change your plans on my behalf.'

'I already have, to an alarming degree, but I shan't this time. The Manor will be vacant, except for servants, if you and your mother would like to come while your own cottage is being put to rights.'

'I hope that is not why you are going?'

'Not at all. That has nothing to do with it. It is only that you will not like to go to Oakdene now, after turning Everett off. He is a pattern card of civility and generosity, but even his good nature must be strained at that.'

'We'll stay home.'

'As you wish. If you change your mind after your first bout of anger with Everett passes, pray feel free to come. I shall leave word with my people you may be coming.'

'Are you taking Ralph with you too?'

'Yes.'

'How long do you plan to stay?' I asked.

'Till my six-weeks' interim custody period has lapsed. Then I must make a visit to London.'

'There should be no difficulty now. I am withdrawing my suit. They are yours. I shall miss them,' I said, already feeling the first pang of loss. How dull and quiet it would be with them gone. Menrod going too. His visits were not always welcome, but they were a lively diversion. Even Mr Everett would decrease the frequency of his visits, though he would not stop them altogether.

'You may miss them so much you want them after all. Odd you did not think to accuse me of that trick, instead of inventing a different one. That sets you thinking, I see.'

'Don't aggravate me. Be firm with Gwen, Menrod. Don't let her get the bit in her teeth, or you'll never control her. And about Ralph – don't be *too* hard on him. He is only a baby still. Oh, I miss him already!'

'If you find the parting unbearable, come to visit us. My house on Marine Parade is large enough to house us all. Then you can see for yourself I am neither a tyrant nor a fool.'

'It is an odd time to be going to Brighton. You more usually go after the London Season, do you not? It will be chilly there in early April, too early to enjoy swimming.'

'We are not going to swim, but to relax, unwind, do some thinking. There is this great emotional sea roiling all around us that must be calmed.'

'I hope you have a pleasant holiday,' I said, arising to find my mother and go home.

'I expect it will be grueling and unpleasant. My best hope is that it will be effective. You are not rid of us just yet, however. I shall take the children to the cottage tomorrow to take their leave of you.'

He ordered our carriage, got Mama away from the card room, and stayed with us till we left, chatting at the door. I went straight home and wrote my notice for the newspaper, and gave it to Pudge to take into town that very night. My mother was nonplussed.

'What is the hurry, Gwendolyn? Surely it can wait till morning.'

'They work all night, setting up the paper. I want it in tomorrow's news. We have left the horses standing ready outside.'

'Sleep on it, dear.'

'I won't sleep till it is finished, once for all.'

'Commune with your heart upon your bed before taking such a giant step,' Mrs Pudge cautioned. She and Pudge would not dream of going to bed before seeing us up the stairs, if we stayed up till dawn, and it was not far from it by then.

'I have communed with my heart till I am tired of it.'

'You'll never get another such offer,' Mama warned.

'I should hope not.'

'Like the daughters of Israel,' Mrs Pudge told her. 'Their daughters were not given to marriage either. A harvest of old maids is what we'll have on our hands, with a plague and a pestilence thrown in, after this night's work.'

'You never had a good word to say for Everett,' I reminded her.

'At least he didn't steal away my Lady, like *some* heathens we could name. Run along, then, Pudge, and post her notice, if she insists on making a parable of herself. We'll not get our ears on our pillows till dawn as it is. I hope I'm not expected to have breakfast on the table at eight in the morning.'

'Sleep till noon if you like,' I offered wildly. 'I plan to.'

The notice was written and taken to Reading that same night. A good thing it was, too. Everett's engagement to Lady Althea was printed directly below it in the morning paper. He had taken me at my word that I would free him immediately. What a fool I would have looked had Althea beat me to the paper with her notice. We learned of the two announcements long before noon. The men began their hammering on the roof at eight.

'Like a bottle in the smoke,' was Mrs Pudge's obscure comment when she read the two notices. 'This will be a wonder unto many. The town will be alive with it. We'll never live it down. It would take a prince on a white charger, at least, to redeem you from this shameful misery.'

An earl in a smart black traveling carriage did not do the trick, but he diverted her flow of venom, at least. Gwen and Ralph were with him, the former looking sulky but dutiful.

'Your niece has something to say to you, Gwendolyn,'

Menrod said, with a commanding look at the girl.

'I'm sorry, Aunt,' she said, her lip quivering. 'I behaved badly, but Mama *did* let me see her and Papa dance in India, didn't she, Ralph?'

'I don't remember,' Ralph answered, looking every bit as downcast as his sister. 'Uncle Menrod is taking us out in his sailboat,' he added, brightening at the prospect. 'I am not afraid. I won't have to swim, because the water is too cold,' he added artlessly.

'I'm not afraid to swim,' Gwen had to boast. 'Can we stay till it is warm enough to swim, Uncle?'

'Not that long, I'm afraid.'

Conversation was difficult, with the noise on the roof. 'Are you quite sure you would not like to spend the next few days at the Manor?' Menrod asked, directing his words to my mother. She was upset at the idea.

'Oh, no, we are perfectly comfortable here,' she assured him, her face wincing at every blow that descended from above.

She held in her hands the newspaper with the two announcements. I noticed Menrod glance at it from time to time, and feared she would bring them to his attention. The visit was short, a formality only, or at least was turned into one, owing to the noise. I worked myself up to a smile for Gwen, which took some doing. Dissatisfied with this meager token of affection, she threw herself into my arms for a bout of sobbing. 'I *am* sorry, Aunt. Truly I am, but it was such a disappointment not to see you dancing. I looked forward to it so. You looked very pretty last night, just like Mama.'

She had the knack of disarming you by these flattering outbursts. I hugged her briefly. 'Monkey,' I chided, laughing in spite of myself. It was Ralph's turn for a farewell embrace. He felt so terribly small in my arms. I knew his fear of the water, and wanted to tell Menrod not to force him into the sailboat if he was too frightened. While the children made their adieux to their grandmother, I mentioned it to him.

'It is best to overcome his fear while he is young. He is pleasantly excited about the sailing. Later in the summer, when he sees Gwen swimming, he will try that too. If Peter and Hettie had known how to swim, they might be alive today. Several of the party made it safely to shore. They were less than a mile from it when the ship sank.'

'I thought you were staying only a short time!'

'I usually return to Brighton after the Season is over,' he answered. It filled me with desolation. I had pictured them all coming back after the visit was up. This was how life would be in the future. They would be darting all over the country, seldom settled in at the Manor, as they had been the past weeks.

'Of course. I had forgotten,' I said.

The children had finished hugging Grandma goodbye. They stood, waiting for the word to leave. 'We're off,' Menrod said, in a hearty spirit. 'Say goodbye to the plants for me, Gwendolyn. Take good care of them, and yourself.'

There was a knock on the cottage door. I was dismayed to see Mr Everett enter before Menrod and the children had got away. I would now be subjected to some heavy-handed roasting by the two gentlemen. Menrod turned a satirical eye toward me. He read the unhappiness on my face.

'Good morning, Mr Everett. We are just off to Brighton. Congratulations on your engagement,' was all he said, but it revealed he had read the paper before coming.

'Thankee kindly, Menrod. I see you have already read the news. I have five or six papers here to leave off with friends who have not seen it. It is a big day for me. The racket on the roof must be deafening you all,' he shouted, to make himself heard above it.

'Not at all. We are used to it,' I said.

' 'Tis a friendly sound after all, the blow of a hammer on wood,' he agreed.

'We'll settle up the bill when I return,' Menrod told him.

'You'll be wanting the ceiling in the bedchamber plastered as well? I have a lad. . . .'

'If you would be so kind.'

'Happy to oblige you,' he said, then they passed each other in the hallway, Menrod and the children to leave, Everett to come in.

'You have taken us by surprise, Mr Everett,' Mama said, not happy, nor pretending to be, at the nature of the surprise.

'I am the most surprised of the lot. It fair bowled me over,' he told her humbly. 'I never thought, when she came trotting down to Oakdene every two days, what she had in her mind. A dozen times she told me how happy I must be, surrounded by so many lovely things, lacking only a wife to complete my joy. I thought it was a roasting about Gwendolyn, but it was no such a thing. It was herself she pictured there all the time. She out and out said as much last night. Yessir, it fair knocked me down. I wasn't tardy to offer her the ring. It looks very handsome on her dainty white fingers, if I do say so myself. You know the ring, Gwendolyn – Miss Harris,' he said, slipping back to my more formal name.

'You will get right to work filling up your nursery,' I said. It was the oddest thing, but I felt a spasm of jealousy, to think of Lady Althea having all those objects, which I did not even want. A dog in the manger is what I felt like.

'We won't waste a minute. The wedding is to take place next week, at her home. We're going there shortly. Her folks will want to have a look at me. She'll not be wanting a dozen wee ones, but quality is important, too, as we agreed between us last night. They'll be good stock, half blue-blood,' he said, shaking his head and winking with delight.

It was difficult to get a word in edgewise. He was so overwhelmed with his catch he rattled on nonstop. 'I never thought I'd see the day I would be squire to a titled lady. I never aimed so high. It's a strange thing, surely, she wanted me, but so it is, and I'm not the one to argue. We see pretty well eye to eye on matters. She tells me I have an aristocratic disdain for public gossip and so on. I told her I don't know where I got it, then, unless it rubbed off onto me from herself, for my pa was a woodcutter.'

Her compliment would have been employed to get the announcement in this morning's paper. I think it was aristocratic cunning that accounted for it, myself. He chatted for half an hour before taking his leave. I went with him to the door.

'We'll be seeing you at our ball, if not before. It will not be held till we return from her father's place, the earl, you know,' he added with relish. 'There will be a brace of lords and ladies back home with us after the wedding. It will be good to have some life at Oakdene.'

A honeymoon sounded a strange time to fill the house with guests, but it would not bother Everett. How happy he would be, having throngs of bluebloods to take on a tour of his home. When my resentment of the match wore off, I knew I would think it an excellent one for him – for them both. She would tame him down, steer him through the shoals of high society, introduce him to the fashionable ways of spending his money.

'I'll give the lads their final instructions before I go. Don't think I mean to leave you with your roof half off. Nothing of the sort. Menrod is off to Brighton, did he say?' he asked, at the doorway.

'Yes, he is taking the children there for a holiday,'

'You might very well use that to gain control of them, Miss

Harris,' he said, with a meaningful nod.

'What do you mean? There is nothing wrong in his taking them there.'

'Seems to me he ought to have left them home, when he is off to visit his light o' love. It is Brighton he sent Mrs Livingstone to, is it not? It is what Lady Althea told me, at any rate. If you want to know a secret, it is Mrs Livingstone that kept her from accepting Menrod. He refused to part with the woman. "He cannot have cared for your happiness as much as I do, then," I told her. Not a lie either. I would never treat my wife so shabby.'

He went out, smiling and hitting the half dozen newspapers against the side of his leg. I noticed, as he mounted into his waiting curricle, that his knees did bend; the right one, at least, he bent at forty-five degrees to mount into his buggy.

My mother had not overheard the remark about Mrs Livingstone, and I did not wish to bring it to her attention, but I could not root it out of my own mind. It was a logical explanation for the unseasonable holiday by the sea. I placed no reliance on Lady Althea's claim that Mrs Livingstone had kept her and Menrod apart. It was an excuse for having failed to attach him, a puffing off of her charms to Everett.

It was difficult to think, with the barrage of blows from above and the barrage of wrath from Mama and Mrs Pudge. I was a fool and worse, to have let Everett slip through my fingers. I thought I was too good for him, but *Lady* Althea Costigan, an earl's daughter, did not hold herself so high. Oh, no, *she* knew what she was about, none better. 'She's got the fine art of nabbing a husband down to a science,' Mrs Pudge proclaimed. All day long the maledictions continued, taking on a pseudo-religious fervor after Mrs Pudge spent half an hour with her psalter.

'Our inequities are gone over our heads,' she told me, with a frown at the noisesome roof.

'They certainly are,' I agreed.

'I'm talking about Mr Everett and that woman, the slyest creature ever set her toe into our neighborhood. If there's any relief for you in it, all deadly enemies will be enclosed in their own fat.'

'I do not have any deadly enemies, thank you, fat or otherwise.'

'Money is what it means, miss. It is plain gold that ever made a boney fide lady like Lady Menrod's cousin to marry that common cit. She'll drown in gold.'

'It sounds a pleasant way to go.'

'And *you* will wither like a leaf on the bough.'

'Thank you for reminding me of my plants. I have not watered them today.'

I escaped to the haven of my conservatory, to ruminate in peace and quiet, for even the hammering on the roof was less bothersome here, on the far side from where the men worked. I had soon put all thought of Everett and Lady Althea from mind, for they were not at all important to me. What I disliked very much was Menrod's duplicity in whisking the children off to Brighton so that he might be with his mistress. Did I have a moral obligation to bring it to Mr Doyle's attention, to try in earnest to gain custody of them? Did I have any chance whatsoever of succeeding, and also importantly, did I want them, considering Gwen's nature? After much lengthy consideration, I came up with a negative reply to all questions.

Many, perhaps most, wealthy bachelors had dealings with women before they married. Such behavior would not be considered so grossly immoral as to override Menrod's other qualifications. He would be discreet enough to keep the children away from Mrs Livingstone, or even from rumors of her. He cared for them more than I had imagined he would. He went to the personal bother of teaching Ralph to ride, and now to cure him of his fear of the water. Gwen was a demanding girl, who would always be looking up the hill to the Manor, comparing her situation at the cottage with what it might be there. She would not settle in happily with us.

It sounds foolish to say, but in my heart I think I loved Ralph too much to be at all strict with him. He touched a chord in my heart, touched it so deeply I could not reprimand him, push him, as a growing boy ought to be pushed. Menrod was better at it. I would turn him into a sissy. The courts would not decide in my favor; I knew it as well as I knew anything, so what was the point worrying about it? I asked myself. Yet the worries stayed with me, my constant companions.

I assuaged my conscience in every way I could. I would not abandon the children; I would be as much with them as I could, whenever they were in residence at the Manor. They would spend days, perhaps whole weeks, with me and Mama, on occasions when Menrod was away. He was often away, as he was now, with Mrs Livingstone. . . .

Water splashed down the front of my gown. Coming to attention, I saw I had watered my poor dracaena till it was floating, the water coursing down the sides of the pot, onto the floor. I took myself severely to task. Forget about the children. They will deal fine with their uncle. He won't spoil them, and he won't be cruel. He was fair in his dealings. Oh, but was it fair for him to tell me he was beginning to hate me? Yes, that was what was at the bottom of my turmoil. That was why I could not put Mrs Livingstone out of my mind. I felt betrayed at the knowledge he had gone to her.

I thought he had gone to Brighton to get away from me, because he was becoming too fond of me. He did not want to fall into Peter's trap of marrying a country girl, only from being too much in her company. Such was my opinion of my country-bred charms that I did not think the cure would take. I thought he knew it too, when he invited me to join them in Brighton. I likened his case to a gout victim, who knows it is the rich food and wine that defeats him, yet he must have them in spite of himself. What a fool I would have made of myself had I gone.

So I sat quietly at home, receiving a couple of calls from Lady Menrod, who was bored, with her houseguest gone. The weekly card party at the cottage continued. We read the wedding report of Lady Althea and Mr Everett in the newspapers. They would not be holding their ball for some time; they were off to several countries on their wedding trip. He never can be satisfied with only one of things. There was the trip to Reading on Saturdays, church on Sundays, and a long, desolate week between, to be got in somehow. The roof was mended and rethatched. Mama's ceiling was replastered. My dracaena died from overmothering, and I bought an exotic gardenia to replace it, and to raise my spirits. I usually dug my plants up from the ground around the cottage. The gardenia in bloom had a beautiful aroma. It sat in state on a stone table. I looked at it until I knew every white waxen petal by heart, then the bloom turned brown and fell off. I was happy to be rid of it. It was out of place in my simple garden. As out of place as a romance with Lord Menrod in my simple life.

# Chapter Nineteen

*T*he last few days before Menrod's arrival home with the children were the hardest to bear. He wrote once, a brief business letter to my mother, announcing he would be home after the custody hearing in London. My heart stopped beating when the letter arrived. I thought he was urging us to go to Brighton, but my name was not once mentioned in it. Mrs Pudge said waspishly she would be glad when my eggs had hatched, for if ever she saw a broody hen, it was me, ready to cackle and snap at everyone. To atone for her impertinence, she brought me a disgusting concoction of whipped milk and eggs, flavored with sugar and vanilla.

'For you are too young to go off in your looks, miss,' she felt obliged to add. 'Peaked – you are looking peaked. It comes of losing Mr Everett, but you'll nab a better man yet, if I know anything. They'll all have to drink the wine of astonishment at your catch.'

Menrod had taken the children to Brighton in mid-April, to remain till May. From there, he would go on to London to hear the Court's decision, then bring the children home, but the precise day of his arrival was uncertain. A subtle questioning of Lady Menrod on one of her visits told us he did not plan to linger in London at all, but was coming straight home. As the day of the hearing drew near, I found my nerves growing irritable. I checked the red brick house on the Kennet River each

Saturday to see if Mrs Livingstone had returned. When I saw the knocker back on the door, and the shutters off on my last trip, I knew she had been sent home a few days early, to be ready to receive Menrod.

With so little to occupy my mind, I spent, say wasted, considerable time figuring the exact details of his movements. London is approximately forty miles from the Manor. I knew from Mr Doyle the case was to be heard at ten in the morning. With no opposition, it should be over before noon. They would leave for home shortly after luncheon, to arrive close to dinnertime. He was too polite to arrive at our door at that gauche hour. He would come the next morning. They would all be tired from their exertions.

All my figuring was in vain. They arrived a day early, at three o'clock in the afternoon. The children looked well, their color improved from the sea holiday and their forms filled out somewhat. They ran forward to greet Mama and me. The length of the visit had already caused a change in them. Ralph was less backward, Gwen more subdued. My nephew rattled on excitedly about his sailing, without once mentioning he was not afraid of it, thus convincing me he had overcome his dread of the water. Gwen had ceased collecting things, and spoke instead of social triumphs.

'I met the Prince Regent,' she boasted happily. 'He is very fat, but he lives in a beautiful palace, Aunt, nicer than Mr Everett's house.'

'Did you indeed meet the Prince Regent?' Mama asked, greatly impressed.

'Yes, and he said I was a pretty little thing,' she answered.

'What is his Pavilion like?' Mama asked them.

'It is the style to say it looks as though St Paul's had gone to sea and whelped,' Menrod told her, 'but if so, I would claim the Taj Mahal as the sire. The dome is somewhat oriental in flavor.

The arches and pillars at the east front owe something to the pavilion on the Court of Lions at the Alhambra, the whole of it covered in white icing and plastered with gilt trim by a French pastry cook. Quite abominable.'

'I loved it,' Gwen said.

'So did I,' Menrod admitted, with a boyish smile, 'but it is more sophisticated to find it in poor taste. You would have enjoyed the gardens, Gwendolyn. In the ten acres of grounds, there was hardly a thing in bloom. It quite took me back to your green lean-to. How are your old friends, the plants, progressing? I hope I find them *en bonne santé?*'

'Fine, the same as usual.'

'I helped Captain Jonker lift the anchor. It was very heavy,' Ralph told us. 'He isn't a real Navy captain, but I call him Captain, and he calls me Admiral.'

'We ran aground near Newhaven,' Gwen said. 'It means we got stuck on the bottom of the ocean, on a sandbar.'

'Hush, now, you are only to tell the *good* things,' Menrod warned, in a playful way. 'Your aunt might be interested to hear how you both conquered your *mal de mer.*'

I was more interested to hear the foreign phrases dropping from his lips, indicating some lack of ease.

'We went to church every Sunday,' Gwen offered. 'The weekend Uncle went to London, Miss Enberg took us. She is staying in Brighton till her brother takes her back to India.'

'Miss Enberg is the lady who looked after the children in India last year,' Menrod mentioned.

'Uncle thinks she looked like you, Aunt, but *I* don't think she does,' Gwen said, scrutinizing my face for a similarity. 'She's younger.'

'Only the good things, if you please,' I reminded her.

'We took Miss Enberg out on our ship,' Ralph said, in a proprietary way. 'She wants to get her sea legs back, before she has to go to India.'

'Everett's men did a good job on the roof, I trust?' Menrod asked. 'Did they think to clean the chimney while they were about it? That was the reason for all the catastrophe.'

'They did, and a large bird's nest was in it,' Mama told him. 'It must have been made last summer when we were not using the grate. There were no birds or eggs in it. It was last autumn the chimney took to smoking so dreadfully.'

'Would you care for a cup of tea?' I asked the company.

This was greeted with enthusiasm by everyone. 'I'll step outside and look at the new thatching while it is being made, if you will excuse me a moment, ladies,' Menrod said.

I thought he might invite me to go with him, to allow a few private words, but he did not. There was some constraint in the conversation, after the month's interval.

'So you enjoyed your visit,' Mama said, smiling tenderly on the children. 'Did you have lots of sweets, Gwen?'

'We had ices on the Steyne three times. Mrs Livingstone showed us where the stall is. She lives there.'

'Mrs Livingstone?' Mama asked, her ears perking at the familiar name. 'You never mean *she* was there!'

'Yes, she lives in Promenade Grove.'

'Did you go to visit her?' Mama asked, scandalized.

'No, we met her sometimes on the Steyne.'

Mama and I exchanged a meaningful look. It was not necessary, or possible, to say anything. Our minds were alike enough that we were both revolted to hear Menrod had presented his mistress to his charges. I should have pressed on to win custody of the children. This was wretched behavior on his part. I did not know what I would say, when he returned.

As we still had the young audience to consider, what I said was, 'I am surprised to see you today, Menrod. Is this not the day of the hearing in Chancery?'

'No, it has been delayed a week. Gwen mentioned that I was in London last weekend. When I got news of the delay, I went to try to push it forward on schedule, but a couple of the magistrates have the flu, and all cases are put back. Rather than wait so long at Brighton, we decided to come home and wait here.'

'*I* didn't want to come home,' Ralph said clearly, and received a repressive stare from his uncle.

'The children are missing their ponies,' he added.

'I love Brighton,' Gwen insisted. 'It was Uncle Menrod who wanted to come home.'

His color was high, his manner flustered. I was not surprised to hear him say, '*Soyez sages,*' to the children. Remembering the brass knocker reinstalled on Mrs Livingstone's door, I wondered if she had been sent ahead before he heard of the delay of the case.

'No doubt there was a good reason your uncle wanted to return to the country, when the Season is in full swing in London. I would have thought you would prefer to wait out the week in the city.'

Mrs Pudge came in with the tea tray, to save him from inventing some excuse. 'I didn't expect you today, my dears, or I would have had something special made up for you,' she told the children. 'There's half a dozen of my little tarts left from yesterday. Try some of them.'

The half dozen tarts disappeared rapidly. As soon as they were gone, the children decided they would go out to the swing. 'Don't forget the basket in the carriage, Uncle,' Gwen called as she left.

We looked to learn what the basket might contain. It sounded like a gift, some fruit or fowl from the Manor. We were not accustomed to such perquisites.

'I'll get it now,' he said. 'May I speak to you a moment in private first, Mrs Harris?' he said to my mother.

My curiosity grew higher. What on earth could be in the basket, that required a private word with Mama? It was more usual for him to seek me out for any private matter, as he knew she was not at ease with him. He could surely see how she stared in consternation at his suggestion.

'I shall be in the conservatory when you are through,' I said.

The conservatory gave me a view of the walk to the stable, where the basket would have to be picked up. For five minutes I stood looking out the window, hidden by the screen of cascading ivies, but Menrod did not pass by. My mind was seething with conjecture. In the end, I could think of nothing else but that he was going to marry Mrs Livingstone. He was embarrassed to tell me to my face, and was telling my mother, explaining to her the details. That would be why the children had met her a few times, to see how they all went along together. Before I saw Menrod, I spotted Gwen running up from the stable with the basket. She gave it to him, and he turned toward my conservatory, planning to enter by that door, where he knew he would find me alone. Was it a plant he had got for me?

At the next instant, Mama was at the other door, staring as though she had run mad. 'Gwendolyn, I cannot believe it. He wants to get married! What do you think of that?'

'I am not surprised. I half suspected as much,' I said, my voice loud and clear, my insides shaking.

'Mrs Livingstone right there in Brighton, seeing him every day. And now he has brought the hussy back here. I am sure I did not say a word that made any sense. He is going to speak to you now. Say whatever you think is best, Gwendolyn,' she told me, then fled as the door from the outside opened to permit Menrod to enter.

I was still in confusion as to what the basket had to do with it. It was a large straw affair, with a lid over it. He opened the lid, to reveal Lady and a litter of six kittens, four black, one white, and one spotted.

'Everett would approve of this one,' he said, laughing. 'Six at a crack. He'd fill up his nursery in no time. So did my Tom approve of her, it seems. I doubt the termagant will. Pretty little things, aren't they?' he asked, lifting the white kitten in his hand to admire it. 'All that caterwauling you were subjected to was worth it. How can making love be wrong, when such beauty results? A baby anything is always beautiful. A kind of miracle, really.'

'Where did you find them?' I asked, hardly listening. I was too overwhelmed at Mama's news.

'In the hayloft at the Manor. They're a week or so old, I think. Their eyes are all opened. The kittens are becoming frisky. Lady eloped on you, made a runaway match of it. I like to think they did it legally, over the anvil at the smitty's shop in Reading. Why should Gretna Green get all our business?'

He was in a frivolous mood, as becomes a groom-to-be. I tried to quell down my rage, to be polite. 'I'll give the basket to Mrs Pudge,' I offered. Her steps were heard, running toward us.

'Is it true what the kiddies told me? She's come home?' she asked, running breathless through the door, her topknot completely tumbled to the side of her head.

'Like the human race, she has decided to increase and multiply and fill the earth,' Menrod said, handing her the basket and the one kitten he held in his hand.

She accepted the kitten, held it up till it was about a foot from her nose. 'If that isn't a caution!' she exclaimed. 'The image of Lady. Where is her mama?'

She rooted in the basket for the dame, who meowed proudly at her litter. 'You're a bad girl. Yes, you are,' Mrs Pudge said, but there was no rancor in her. She was won over by the happy family. 'What is to be done – six new mouths to feed, and us with not but a quart of milk in the pantry. Pudge!' She turned to flap from the room, then came back to thank Menrod very cordially.

'Here I was afraid she would break my teeth in my mouth, strike me in the hinder parts, purge me with hyssop, and perform those other cordialities proposed against us sinners in her favorite book.' He stopped talking, looked at me closely. 'What's the matter?' he asked suddenly.

'Nothing.'

'When I left, you were ready to blossom. I even fed you with tepid tea before leaving. You ought to be in bloom by now, instead of. . . .'

'Do I look so hagged?'

'No, you look – vulnerable,' he answered, choosing his word with care. 'Not so vivacious and capable as I have been remembering you. The setting is not to blame. I most often thought of you here, watering pot in hand, chastising the greenery.'

'Menrod, about Mrs Livingstone,' I said, cutting into his speech. It was not the sort of introduction I expected to his announcement. His manner was too intimate. There was admiration in the eyes observing me. Oh, if he was going to marry a nobody, why couldn't it be *me*?

'Did that curst Gwen tell you we met her at Brighton?'

'She mentioned it.'

'She is there for the Season, with her new patron. Lord Havergal has her under his protection. We met her twice on the Steyne. It was impossible to cut her. We were too good friends for that, in the past. We chatted for five minutes – that's all. After the second meeting, I was careful to change our hour for walking there.'

'I thought – I thought she was back here,' I said, rapidly revising my intended utterance, as I realized what misunderstanding had occurred. 'The shutters are off the brick house.'

'You cannot have thought I sent her back here, at such a time! It has been rented to a doctor from Brighton, a fellow I met, who was moving to the neighborhood. He tended Ralph when he had a bout of sniffles. Nothing serious. But about Mrs Livingstone – naturally that part of my past must bother you.'

Why should it bother me unless . . . I had been correct all along. He had gone to Brighton to be cured of hating me, and the cure had not taken.

'There never was a *string* of ladies, stabled across the country, as you accused me of having. It is your friend Everett who indulges in such excesses. I never had but one at a time, and often none.'

'For how many hours?' I asked, laughing for joy.

'*Weeks* at a time. Even months. Well you know yourself how often I ever visited Mrs Livingstone. She was more a Platonic friend than anything else. Practically.'

'You poor deprived creature! Here I have gone twenty-five years without a single lover.'

'It's time we did something about that,' he said, sweeping me into his arms. I had a sensation – it could only have been a memory – of the sweet aroma of the gardenia, heady and exciting, almost intoxicating in its richness, surrounding me, there in the greenhouse. It was a fleeting impression, soon lost in stronger sensations as I felt the bruising pressure of his lips, the close clutch of his arms around me, the increased beat of my heart, and his against it. It was a violent, almost a frightening first brush with love, but his words, and his eyes, were gentle when he released me.

'That will teach you to make fun of me,' he said. 'Twenty-five years, eh? We have got a lot of catching up to do.'

'There is no hurry,' I said. My senses wanted a respite.

'I've got the whole day free. We can take our time.' He

kissed me again, with enough ardor to frighten me half to death, and enough gentleness to guide me through the hazardous undertaking.

All good things must come to an end. I reluctantly detached myself from his arms. 'Did I tell you I got a gardenia?' I asked, to draw his attention to another direction.

'You are branching out from weeds, are you? I hope this doesn't mean you have been making up to that botanist from Reading during my absence.'

'I still have not met him. The gardenia died, and it was very pretty, too.'

He looked at the brown petals, sitting in the pot. 'A berry is forming. See? The flower must wither, to make way for the fruit. More flowers will come if you take care of it.'

'I will. I am planning a more adventurous garden in the future.'

'Leave plenty of time to tend your Menrod cactus. We bloom too, if properly nurtured.'

He behaved more like a clinging ivy than a prickly cactus. 'Where do you want to be married, here or in London?' he asked, drawing my arm around his waist. 'We'll have to be in the city next week for the hearing. We could introduce you then, take in the remainder of the Season, if you like.'

'What about the children?'

'I know you will want them with you. I have been at pains to trim Gwen into line and urge Ralph a little out of it. It was a sticky month, without you there to give me a hand. We had many a bout of tears, and threats she would run home to Aunt Harris, but I laid down some hard ground-rules, and she is shaping up. The job is by no means done, mind you. We must set our course, and sail it together. She is quick to find out our weaknesses. *I* won't give in to her against your wishes, and vice versa. It is the only way to handle her. That Miss Enberg – not a clever woman. Hardly a woman at all, in fact, but only a young girl, which is perhaps how Gwen got so far out of line.'

'Our being at odds put her in a good position. She was quick to wiggle through any little wedge between us.'

'United we stand, as the Americans say. I personally don't intend to allow an inch between you and me, at any time. I am not speaking only about Gwen and her tricks, either. She is so forward she'll be married within a fortnight. She very nearly got an offer from Prinny last month. Truly, though, we won't be saddled with her forever.'

'We'll be losing Ralph long before that, when he goes off to school. The house will seem strange and empty without them.'

'Devil a bit of it. We'll have half a dozen of our own by then. Everett is not the only one who appreciates your breeding potential. Which brings us back to my first question – when and where shall we be married?'

'I would like to have it done in my father's old church, with the rector, Mr Miles, officiating. He would like to do it, and Mama will not want to go all the way to London. She dislikes travel.'

'I hope you don't. There are so many things I want to show you – mountains and rivers and temples. It would be the deuce of a bother to have them hauled to Reading. I'll drop by now and see Miles. If we skip the banns and use a license, we could be married before we have to go to London. Any objections?'

'It doesn't leave me much time to prepare my bridal clothes. . . .'

'Althea did it up in a week. If I know anything, her bridal clothes will be ten times as fine and as numerous as yours. Couldn't you just buy a new shawl, or something, and leave the rest of it to get in London? Not that I am anxious for your company, you understand! But if you refuse, I shall drag you into Reading and have the smitty perform the nuptials, as he did for Lady and Tom.'

I sensed the eagerness, amounting almost to anxiety, beneath the frivolous words. 'A pity the cure in Brighton did not take, Menrod. I know you went to cure yourself of liking me, but you know absence makes the heart grow fonder as often as it puts out of mind what is out of sight. Had you remained here, you would be tired of me by now.'

'I hope you don't think *that* is why I went!' he exclaimed.

'Wasn't it?'

'Certainly not! You told me you would not share a roof with Gwen, after her performance at the ball. I went to bring her to heel so we could begin our marriage with some semblance of peace and order. Bad enough to have to start off with Peter's children, without having one of them driving us to distraction with her tantrums. I wanted to get her away from all her spoilers. I thought you understood that. I would have been more explicit, but you remember your mother chose that one morning I left to bear us company. Then Everett landed in just as we were about to have a moment alone at the door. Gwendolyn, is that really what you thought?' he asked, frowning.

'You *did* tell Mama the only reason Peter married my sister was because he found himself alone in the country, with no *decent* company.'

'What have Peter and Hettie to do with *us*? He was a green boy, had never been anywhere. I have been half way around the world, sampling, *by sight!* the ladies of all the countries. I know what I am doing, know what I want, and I want you. Is that why my flower has wilted?' he asked, drawing a finger along my cheek. He looked genuinely sorry.

'I would not have troubled you so for worlds. I thought you *knew*, as surely as *I* knew you had had the misfortune to fall in love with me, that I couldn't live without you. If Peter had the temerity to say it to me, I guess I can use the overblown phrase too. I'll make it up to you. What can I do?'

'I'll have a lifetime to pay you back. It would be nice if Mama could be happy too. The box stairs. . . .'

'I knew you wouldn't make it easy for me! Even – to show the depths of my chagrin – I will allow the desecration of this gem of Elizabethan architecture. The box stairs will be renovated, temporarily, for the duration of your mother's stay here. We'll put the wall panels back on as soon as she is through with the cottage, however.'

'She kept the brass railings, and the panels with the gilded. . . . Were the white panels and gilt roses not included?' I asked, as he looked unhappy. 'I was *very* miserable while you were gone, knowing you were in Brighton with Mrs Livingstone.'

'Here I have been blaming Hettie for Gwen's tricks! She inherited them from *you*! Well, perhaps if you ask me *very* nicely.'

'She is a poor widow,' I pointed out, with an abject face. 'If Papa were alive, he would let her have them.'

'All right. I know when I'm outclassed, but don't think this sets the tone for our future. There will be no crimson stair-runner. I whipped Gwen into line, and if this continues, it is the Brighton cure for you, miss. Furthermore, that was *not* what I meant by asking nicely. I meant *this*,' he said, pulling me into his arms.

Also by Joan Smith
and soon to be published:
BATH BELLES

---

IT IS HIGH TIME FOR BELLE TO FACE FACTS – HER
FIANCÉ IS DEAD AND *HER* LIFE MUST GO ON.

When Belle Haley finally arrives to inspect the London
house that her dead Graham bequethed to her, she can
scarcely wait to sell it and return home to Bath.

But when wealthy insurance tycoon Desmond Maitland
shows an uncommon interest in her impressive abode,
Belle makes some inquiries. It seems Graham was
murdered after retrieving £10,000 of Maitland's insurance
money – a fortune that is still at large!

Is the money still in the house? As Belle, Maitland and
Graham's relations search for clues, Belle learns she has
been mourning a man she never really knew. . . .